Twice Garrett Had Been On The Verge Of Confessing His Identity.

"What about you and marriage?" Sophia asked, breaking into his thoughts.

"I'm a workaholic, I suppose," he said. "I haven't ever been deeply in love, and I don't feel ready for marriage."

As he gazed into her eyes, he wondered what it would be like to come home to her every night—to make love to her night and day. His thoughts surprised him.

He hated not telling her about the Delaneys, yet he had heard the bitterness in her voice when she spoke of her father, felt her anger smoldering.

He realized she was staring at him with a quizzical smile. "What?" he asked.

"You haven't heard one word I've been saying, Garrett. What are you thinking about?"

He focused on her lips before looking into her eyes again while desire consumed him.

He didn't want to admit the truth yet and the burden of guilt was becoming unbearable, but one way to avoid both was to stop her questions with kisses.

Dear Reader,

This second story in the Lone Star Legacy series involves the celebration of two people falling in love in spite of seemingly insurmountable obstacles. Love and romance are wonderful, breathtaking, sometimes overwhelming. The road to romance is a fascinating journey.

Set in glittering Dallas and the snow-covered Rockies, *The Reluctant Heiress* shows how the Delaney brothers discover a half sister who has to be brought into the family. To achieve this goal, the brothers turn to a trusted friend and valued employee, Garrett Cantrell.

The first meeting between the handsome Garrett and striking Sophia Rivers ignites fires in each of them. Sophia cannot resist Garrett even though she knows she should. Trust is fundamental, and forgiveness is a part of Sophia's and Garrett's story.

Some of the most exciting moments in life happen when two people fall in love. Romance is universal, sought after and just plain fun. Come enjoy Garrett's and Sophia's story.

Thank you for choosing this book.

Sara Orwig

SARA ORWIG

THE RELUCTANT HEIRESS

HARLEQUIN®

entertain, enrich, inspire™

Recycling programs
for this product may
not exist in your area.

ISBN-13: 978-0-373-73189-3

THE RELUCTANT HEIRESS

www.Harlequin.com

Printed in U.S.A.

Books by Sara Orwig

Harlequin Desire

Silhouette Desire

Other titles by this author
available in ebook format

SARA ORWIG

lives in Oklahoma. She has a patient husband who will take her on research trips anywhere from big cities to old forts. She is an avid collector of Western history books. With a master's degree in English, Sara has written historical romance, mainstream fiction and contemporary romance. Books are beloved treasures that take Sara to magical worlds, and she loves both reading and writing them.

Many thanks to Stacy Boyd and Maureen Walters.

Prologue

"I don't have a clue why I'm here," Garrett Cantrell, company CFO, said at the family gathering in the Dallas office of Delaney Enterprises.

"Because Sophia Rivers is our father's child. She's as stubborn as Dad ever was," Will Delaney stated, combing his fingers through his black hair.

"We won't give up. There's too much at stake," Ryan Delaney added, resting one booted foot on his knee. "We can be as stubborn as she is. There has to be a way to reach her."

"We need to outsmart her instead of the other way around," Zach Delaney grumbled.

"Right," said Will. "That's why I asked Garrett to join us."

"I'm sure finding out you have a half sister at the reading of your dad's will was a shock," Garrett said, "but you should face the fact that she doesn't want to meet any of you. I'd say give it up."

"If we don't get her on the board of the Delaney Foundation, we can kiss our inheritances goodbye," Zach snapped. "Also, she's family. We have a sister—all these years."

"I agree," Will added. "She's part of our family and we'd all like to know her."

"Even if she doesn't want to know you?" Garrett asked.

"I think that's because of Dad and not anything we've done. We just want to unite this family and we don't stand a chance if she won't speak to us," Will said. "Each of us has tried and failed to make contact with her. I think the next thing is to send someone neutral."

Garrett straightened in his chair, his good humor vanishing. "Go through your dad's lawyer. She communicates with Grady."

"Her attorney communicates with Grady," Will replied drily. "Grady has never met the lady."

"The bottom line is, we want our inheritances," Ryan stated. "She's costing each of us four billion dollars. Too much to blow off."

As Garrett looked at the Delaneys, he reflected on how his life had been tied to theirs from the day he was born. His father's life had been closely linked with the family patriarch, Argus Delaney. Besides ties of work and family, Will Delaney, the Delaney CEO, was Garrett's best friend. Garrett had been raised to feel indebted to the Delaneys, just as his dad had felt obligated. As he thought about what they were about to ask of him, his dread grew exponentially. "I suggest the three of you try again to meet her," Garrett said.

"C'mon, Garrett. You can contact her because your

name isn't Delaney. Spend time with her, get to know her, find out why she's resisting, and we'll take it from there," Will said. "Just open the door for us. Go to Houston. You have a family business and a house there. It's a perfect plan."

"I own the property management business in Houston—I don't work there. Give it up, guys. Don't ask me to do what you can't do."

"We think you *can* do this," Will argued. "You've been our spokesperson many times. We'll make it worthwhile for you. Help us get her on the board and it's another five hundred million for you."

Garrett was already wealthy— He didn't care about the money. But he couldn't turn down the brothers because his obligation to the Delaneys ran deep. He sighed as Will handed him a manila folder.

Garrett looked at a picture of a raven-haired, brown-eyed beauty. *Maybe their request isn't so bad after all,* he thought.

"If she cooperates, she will inherit three billion dollars. It's not like you're trying to cause her trouble," Ryan pointed out.

"How can she turn down that kind of money?" Zach asked, shaking his head.

"She must be angry as hell," Garrett remarked. "That kind of anger isn't going to change easily."

"We have to try," Will stated. "Will you do it?"

Garrett glanced at the picture again. He had just inherited three billion from their father. Will was his closest friend. How could he refuse to help them now?

"Garrett, we're desperate. And we have a time limit," Ryan said.

"All right," Garrett replied reluctantly. "I can't say no to any of you."

There were thanks from all and a high five from Will, who grinned. "Everything's going for you. You're not a Delaney."

"I might as well be one," Garrett grumbled. "I don't think your half sister will be one degree happier with me than she was with any of you." Garrett shook his head. "Meeting Sophia Rivers is doomed from the start."

One

Sophia Rivers sipped champagne and gazed beyond the circle of friends surrounding her. Her small Houston gallery was filled with guests viewing her art and helping her celebrate the second anniversary of her gallery's opening. The crowd was the perfect size, and she was completely satisfied with the turnout.

"Sophia, I have a question."

She turned to see Edgar Hollingworth, a father to her and a mentor, as well as a man whom she and her mother had been friends with before she ever moved into the art world. "Excuse me," she said to the group around her, and stepped away.

"Edgar, what can I do for you?" she said to the tall, thin man.

"You looked as if you needed rescuing," he said quietly. "You also look ravishing. The black and white is striking on you, Sophia."

"Thank you," she replied, shaking her long black hair away from her face.

"Shall we at least act as if I've asked you about a painting?" Edgar motioned toward the opposite side of the room and she smiled as she strolled with him. "You have a sizable crowd tonight. I'm glad you were able to make it. I haven't seen you in a long time."

"I hadn't planned to come until about three hours ago. I've been in New Mexico, painting. Who's the couple ahead to our right?" she asked.

"The Winstons. They're probably on your guest list because they bought a painting recently."

"Now how do you know that?"

"I sold it to them," he said, smiling at her, causing creases to fan from the corners of his blue eyes. "I still think you should move your gallery nearer mine. Our galleries would complement each other."

Sophia smiled at the familiar conversation that always ended with her saying no. "I do appreciate your gallery carrying my art. You were the first and I'll always be indebted to you for that."

"You would have been in a gallery anyway whether it was my place or another's. You have a fine talent."

"Thank you, Edgar," she said.

Sophia glanced around the room again and was slightly surprised when she saw another unfamiliar face. Except this one took her breath away.

Perhaps the tallest man in the room, he stood in profile. His brown hair had an unruly wave to it and his hawk nose and rugged looks made her think instantly that he would be an interesting subject to paint. He held a champagne flute in his hand as he looked at a painting.

"There's someone else I don't know," she said.

"His name is Garrett Cantrell. We talked awhile. He

has a property management business here and he's a financial adviser. He, too, bought one of your paintings last week. Another satisfied customer."

A woman approached Edgar, who excused himself, leaving Sophia to contemplate the tall, brown-haired stranger, strolling slowly around the gallery. She suddenly found herself crossing the room to stand near him.

"I hope you like it," she said.

"I do," he replied, turning to look at her with thickly lashed eyes the color of smoke. Her breath caught. Up close he was even more fascinating—handsome in a craggy way—and his gray eyes were unforgettable.

"That's good," she replied, smiling and extending her hand while still held in his compelling gaze. "Because I'm the artist. I'm Sophia Rivers."

"Garrett Cantrell," he said, shaking her hand. His warm fingers wrapped around hers and an uncustomary tingle ran to her toes. She gazed into his smoke-colored eyes and couldn't get her breath. Her gaze slipped lower to his mouth. She wondered what it would be like to kiss him. The temperature in the room rose. She knew she should look away, yet she didn't want to stop studying him.

"The artist herself. And even more beautiful than your paintings," he said as he released her hand. "You've caught the atmosphere of the West."

"It's New Mexico, around Taos. And thank you," she added. Her pulse jumped at his compliment and she was keenly aware of him as they moved to view another painting.

"You're very good at what you do. I look at these and feel as if I'm there instead of standing in a steamy metropolitan city."

"That's what I hope to achieve. So this is the first time you've been to my gallery."

"Yes, but I own one of your pictures," he said, moving to the next painting. "You must spend a lot of time in New Mexico. I assume you have a gallery there?"

"Actually, I don't. I intend to open one early next year, but I haven't launched into that yet. It will take time away from painting."

"I understand." He sipped champagne and moved to another painting. "Ah, I really like this one," he said and she looked at a familiar work. It was an aged cart in front of a brown adobe house with bright hollyhocks growing around it. A small mesquite tree stood at one corner of the house.

He looked at the next series of paintings. "These are my favorites. The Native American ones," he said, indicating a man with a long black braid standing beside a horse in an open stretch of ground dotted with mesquite. Overhead, white clouds billowed against a blue sky and a large hawk sailed with widespread wings.

"That's a great painting," he said. "The light and shadows are an interesting contrast." Happy with his compliment, she smiled. "I'll take this one. Any chance the artist will help me decide where to hang it? A dinner is in the offering."

Again, she had a flutter in her heartbeat. "We're strangers, Mr. Cantrell."

"It's Garrett. We can fix the 'strangers' part. When you can get away tonight, why don't we go around the corner to the hotel bar and have a drink? Tomorrow evening we'll hang my painting and then I'll take you to dinner."

"You don't waste time. I'd be delighted to have a drink tonight. I should be through here in another hour."

"Excellent," he said, glancing at his watch.

"I'll get one of my staff to wrap your painting and we can deliver it tomorrow if you'd like."

"That will be fine. The delivery person can leave it with my gatekeeper."

She smiled and left to find one of her employees. "Barry, would you help Mr. Cantrell? He wants number 32. Please take care of the sale and get the delivery information."

She had to resist the temptation to glance over her shoulder at Garrett.

Instead, she strolled around, speaking to customers and friends, meeting Edgar again.

"I see Cantrell bought a painting."

"Yes. I'm having a drink with him after this."

"That was quick," he said, glancing across the room. "Seemed nice enough. Wealthy enough, too. Last week he bought your painting from me without hesitation. Now, a week later, he's buying another one. The man knows what he likes."

"I see the Santerros. I have to speak to them."

"Have fun this evening," Edgar said as she left him.

"I intend to," she stated softly. "Garrett Cantrell," she repeated, glancing back to see him at the desk, handing a business card to Barry. Her gaze drifted over his long legs while her heartbeat quickened. Dressed in a navy suit with a snowy dress shirt and gold cuff links, the handsome man was a standout even in the well-dressed crowd.

She spent the next hour all too aware of where Garrett stood.

When she saw him talking to a couple she recognized, she waited until he moved away, then worked her way around to them.

"How are the Trents tonight?" she asked.

"Fine," Jason Trent answered.

"We love your new paintings," Meg Trent said. "Thanks for the invitation."

"Thank you for attending. I saw you talking to Garrett Cantrell. I just met him, but it looked as if you two already know him."

"We do," Jason replied. "I lease a building from his company. He keeps up with whether everything is going smoothly, which it is. Good bunch to work with."

"We're getting one of your watercolors for the family room," Meg said. "It's the one with the little boy and the burro."

"I'm glad you like that one. I hope you enjoy having it in your home."

"You're a prolific painter," Jason remarked.

"I enjoy it."

"More than the financial world," he said, smiling.

"I have no regrets about changing careers."

"That's what I keep trying to talk Meg into doing— She'd love to have a dress shop."

"Accounting seems to hold fewer risks. You're established now, but weren't you nervous when you started?" Meg asked.

"I suppose, but it was absolutely worth it," Sophia said. "It was nice to see you both," she added, moving on, aware of Garrett across the gallery talking to two people. She wondered whether he knew them, too.

She stopped at the desk to look at his card. "Cantrell Properties Inc." It was a plain card with a downtown address, logo and phone number, but little else. She returned it to the drawer.

Garrett appeared at her side. "Can you leave? You still have quite a few people here."

"I can leave. My staff can manage quite well. They weren't expecting me to be here tonight anyway."

"I'm glad you are," he said.

"We can go out the back way and it'll be less noticeable." She led him through a door, down a hallway that opened onto offices, a mailroom and a studio and out the back into a parking lot where five cars were parked. Four tall lampposts illuminated the area as brightly as if it were day. A security guard sat in a cubicle watching a small television. He stepped to the door.

"Good night, Miss Rivers."

"I'll be back after a while to get my car, Teddy."

"Sure thing. Evening, sir," he said, nodding at Garrett who greeted him in return.

"My car is in front," Garrett said, taking her arm.

"It's a nice night. We can walk if you want," she said, pleasantly aware of his height because she was taller than some men she knew and as tall as many.

"I saw you talking to Meg and Jason Trent. Jason said he leased property from you."

"Yes, he's a good tenant," he said. "They like your art."

"I've had a gratifying response from people," she said.

They entered the bright hotel lobby, then the darkened bar where a pianist played a ballad for couples who were dancing.

Garrett got a booth with a small lamp at the end of the table. It spilled a golden glow over his fascinating features, highlighting his prominent cheekbones and leaving the planes of his cheeks in dark shadows. She felt breathless again, a steady hum of excitement that she couldn't explain.

They ordered drinks—a cold beer for him and an

iced soda for her. When they came, he raised his glass in a toast. "Here's to a new friendship. May it grow."

"A toast to friendship," she repeated, touching his cold bottle lightly. She sipped her soda and set the glass down.

He reached across the table to take her hand, his warm fingers enveloping hers. Again, a current streaked through her like lightning. "Shall we dance?"

As she stood, he shed his coat and tie, folding them once on the seat of the booth.

Sophia followed him to the small dance floor and stepped into his embrace. Her hand was in his, her other hand on his shoulder, feeling the warmth of him through the fine cotton shirt. She enjoyed dancing around the floor, aware of how well they moved together. He was agile, light on his feet.

"I've been waiting all evening for this moment," he said, setting her heart fluttering again. She had never had such an instant and intense reaction to a man. "I'm glad I decided to come tonight. I didn't expect to see the artist, but I knew I would enjoy looking at your art. Now, the whole world has changed."

She smiled. "I don't think it's been a world-changing night," she said, though she actually agreed with him. She wasn't sure things would ever be the same after having met Garrett Cantrell.

"The night isn't over yet," he reminded her, obviously flirting.

She slanted him a look. "Perhaps you'll change my mind."

"That's a challenge I'll gladly take."

The ballad ended and a faster number began. Garrett released her and she put a little distance between them. The man had sexy moves that set her pulse at a faster pace. She was unable to tear her gaze from his until she forced herself to turn and the spell was broken.

By the time the music finished, she needed to catch her breath.

Garrett took her hand. "Shall we go back to our drinks?"

They returned to the booth. He loosened the top buttons of his shirt. The temperature climbed a notch and her desire revved with it.

Her cell phone chimed. She looked down, reading a brief text from Edgar.

How is your evening with G.C.? Call me when you get home. I promised Mom.

She had to laugh. "I have a text from my friend Edgar. You bought a painting of mine from him."

"Yes. I remember."

"He once promised my mom that he would look out for me and he's been like the proverbial mother hen ever since. He's checking on when I'll get home."

Garrett flashed a breathtakingly handsome smile. "Is he jealous?"

Shaking her head, she laughed. "Definitely not. Edgar always loved my mother. They dated some, but for Mom it was a good friend sort of thing. Then as my interest in art developed, Mom told Edgar. He became a friend and mentor, helping me in so many ways."

She sent a text back.

Go to bed, Edgar. I'm fine and he's fun.

"I let him know that I'm okay and we're having a pleasant time."

"A pleasant time. I'll have to try harder if I want to move that into the 'world-changing' arena."

She smiled as she put away her cell phone. "So tell me about yourself," she said.

"I grew up with the proverbial silver spoon. Well, my dad began to make big bucks when I was about seven years old. Life was easy in some ways."

"What wasn't easy?"

"My mom died when I was fifteen. My dad and I were close. I lost him this past summer."

"Sorry. It hurts. My mom died a couple of years ago."

"Your dad?"

"I never knew him," she said, her eyes becoming frosty as she answered him.

"I'm glad you and your mom were close. So how did you get into art?"

"It's my first love. I went to college, got a degree in accounting, got a good job, moved up. I began to invest my own money and did so well, I finally took over managing my mother's finances, which was far more than I had. Finance became my field, but art was—and is—my love. We have something else in common—our financial backgrounds."

"So we do."

"The difference is, you love it and pursue it. I wanted something else."

"Sometimes I think about something else, but I'm locked into where I am."

"What else do you think about doing?" she asked.

"Nothing serious. I'm where I should be, doing what I've been trained to do and have a knack for doing."

"There's something else you like," she persisted, tilting her head to study him. "I don't think it's art. I'll bet it's far removed from the world of property management."

"Yes, it is. It's not that big a deal for you to even try to guess. Someday when I retire, I'll make furniture. I like working with my hands."

"It's getting a little scary how alike we are," she said, noticing how his thick lashes heightened the striking effect of his gray eyes.

"Perhaps it's an omen indicating we will get along well."

"Usually, it's the other way around. Opposites attract."

"Well, I'll see where we're opposite—one thing, you're living your dream. I won't leave the business world."

"Why not?"

He shrugged a broad shoulder. "I was raised to do this. When Dad was alive, I wouldn't have changed for anything because it would have hurt him terribly. He hasn't been gone long and I just can't think about changing when I know how badly he wanted me to do what I'm doing. There are other reasons, too, but that's the biggest."

She nodded. "We're different there, all right. My mom was okay with the change I made. I'm sorry she didn't live to see the success I've been lucky enough to have, especially since she's the one who told me to chase my dream."

"Be thankful. I've been told the opposite all my life."

"I am thankful," she said, wondering about his life as the topic of conversation shifted. As she looked at him, desire smoldered, a steady flame. She knew he would kiss her tonight and she wanted him to.

"So there are no other men in your life?" he asked, tilting his head.

"No, no other men and you're not exactly in it either since I've known you all of a few hours."

"I'm in it now," he said in a tone of voice that stirred sparks. "So Mr. Right has not come along. And there's no one vying for that title."

"I'm definitely not looking for Mr. Right. The past few years I've been incredibly busy and my social life has suffered."

"I can understand about incredibly busy. And I'll see what I can do to remedy that a little for both of us."

"And what about the women in your life? You can't convince me there are none."

"There isn't anyone special, or even anyone really 'in' my life at this point. I'm free as a bird, as they say."

"Workaholic?"

"I'm not arguing that one."

When her phone chimed again with a text that the gallery was cleaned and closed, she noticed the late hour. "I didn't know the time. I should go home."

As they walked back to the gallery, Garrett stopped her. "Why don't I take you home? I'll pick you up for breakfast and bring you back to the gallery to get your car."

"That seems a lot of trouble for you."

"No trouble at all," he said, unlocking the door of a black sports car.

After a moment, she climbed in, gave Garrett her address and watched him drive, studying his hands with neatly trimmed nails. A gold cuff link glinted in the reflection of the dash lights.

They drove through a gated area and up the front drive of her sprawling house. He parked and came around to open the door for her. They crossed the porch and she unlocked the door before turning to face him.

"You have a nice home."

"Thanks. As you said, it's comfortable. It's too late to invite you in but I had a great time tonight."

"It's too early to exchange goodbyes," he said, slipping his arm around her waist to draw her close.

Sophia's heart raced as she looked up at him. His lower lip was full, sensual. She leaned slightly closer, pressing against him and closing her eyes as his mouth covered hers lightly, then firmly, his tongue thrusting into her mouth. A wave of longing rippled, tearing at her while she felt as if she were in free fall. Her breathing altered, heat pooled low in her. His kiss was demanding, enticing and she returned it. She moaned softly, the sound taken by his mouth on hers.

Her heart pounded so violently she was certain he could feel it. When she pressed against his lean, hard length, his arm tightened around her. Leaning over her, holding her tightly, he didn't let up. She was lost, consumed in kisses that were magical, that set her on fire.

One hand slipped down her back, a light caress, and the other was warm on the nape of her neck. His kisses were earth-shattering, rocking her world. She had never been kissed this way. She wanted to stay in his arms for hours.

Finally she leaned away to look at him. "Garrett, slow down," she whispered, caution and wisdom fighting to gain control over desire. All she wanted was to kiss him endlessly.

As he gazed at her intently, she realized that his ragged breathing matched her own.

"Sophia," he said, her name a hoarse whisper. "I

want you." The words—stark, honest and direct—set her pulse galloping.

"We have to say good-night," she declared. She had just met him and barely knew him. She should not fall into his arms instantly and lose all control.

Locks of his dark, unruly hair had tumbled on his forehead, escaping the neatly combed style he'd worn when she first saw him. She ached to run her hands through them.

Instead, she took a deep breath and stepped back. "We have to say good-night," she repeated. "I had a wonderful time."

"It was world-changing for me," he whispered, his voice still only a rasp. He framed her face with his hands. "I mean it. Tonight was a special night that I never, ever expected. I'd hoped to meet you but I never once thought I'd have an evening like this." As he spoke, his fingers combed lightly through her hair. His words carried a sincerity that made her heartbeat quicken again, his smoky, intense gaze consuming her.

"I didn't expect anything like this either," she whispered, wanting him with an urgency that shook her.

"When I walked into your gallery, I wanted to meet you for one reason. After meeting you, I want to be with you for an entirely different reason," he said.

He leaned down to kiss her again, passionately. When he released her, he stepped away, but his hand stayed on her shoulder as if he didn't want to break the physical contact with her.

"I'll see you in the morning. How's seven?"

She nodded, and he turned and strode away. She stared at him—broad shoulders, narrow waist, long legs, thick brown hair, handsome. The man took her breath and set her heart pounding.

"Good night, Garrett," she said softly. She closed the door and switched on lights while her lips tingled. Desire was a scorching flame. Garrett Cantrell. She would be with him again in just hours and yet she couldn't wait.

Her cell phone's tune signaled a call. She looked at the number with curiosity as she answered. Her heart missed a beat when she heard Garrett's deep voice.

She laughed. "You do know that we just parted?"

"We did. It now seems like a serious mistake. Tell me more about growing up, your dreams, your day tomorrow."

Smiling, she sat in a rocker in her bedroom, gazing at her shelves of familiar books and pictures. "I grew up in Houston. I've always dreamed of painting and having my own gallery. Tomorrow—"

"Wait a minute. Back up. You grew up in Houston. House? Apartment? Best friends through your school years or did you move a lot? Tell me about your life, Sophia."

When he said her name in his deep drawl, her pulse beat faster. "It can't possibly be that fascinating. I grew up in one house, went to neighborhood elementary schools and then private schools later. I had the same close friends through elementary and then new friends in the private school. See? All very routine and ordinary."

"There is absolutely nothing ordinary about you," he said, stirring another thrilling physical reaction in her that threw her completely off base. She wasn't used to feeling like this because of a man.

"What about you? You said you had it easy growing up?" she asked.

"I always went to private schools. I've had the same

best friend all my life since I was too young to remember. Our fathers were best friends. I've had the same family home my whole life. I'm an only child."

"We're so much alike, I'm surprised we can stand each other, Garrett." When he laughed, she felt her stomach drop, like she was in free fall. He was turning her inside out with just the sound of his voice.

"You're already living your dream. Do you feel fulfilled, complete?" he asked.

"I think people always want more and keep striving. I am very happy with my life, though, and what I do."

"Surely there's something else you want."

"Another successful gallery in Taos. I'd like to live in Santa Fe. But I already have a home and studio, and I have a cabin in the mountains near Questa, where I go for solitude to paint."

"The Questa cabin sounds isolated."

"No cell phone reception whatsoever, which is a plus. I have a caretaker. He and his family have a cabin close to mine, so there are people nearby. He has four dogs. Two take up with me when I'm there, so that's a bit of company. It's a good place to work with no interference—a good place to improve my skills as a painter."

"I'd say you can settle for how well you paint right now."

"No, I can definitely improve. So tell me about you, Garrett. Do you really dream of building furniture someday?"

"It's pushed to a burner so far back, it will take years to get to it."

As they talked, she moved to the window, switching off a lamp and gazing outside at the full moon. By the time she glanced at the clock, she was shocked to see it was half past three.

"Garrett, we have to get off the phone. It's after three a.m., and you're picking me up at seven."

"All right. Sophia, you're a remarkable woman," he said in a solemn tone. She suddenly had a funny feeling that he had expected something different from her.

"And you are a remarkable man," she replied softly. "Good night, Garrett. I will see you soon—very soon."

"Night, Sophia," he said, and was gone.

She turned off her phone and crawled into bed, Garrett dominating her thoughts completely. "Garrett," she whispered, enjoying saying his name while she thought about his magical kisses. She had never expected to meet someone like him tonight. This wasn't a time in her career to be distracted, yet he made her feel things she had never felt before. Morning couldn't come quickly enough. She was already anxious to be with him again.

Two

Setting aside his phone to strip to his briefs, Garrett replayed the night, thinking of the first moment he had seen Sophia at the gallery. In high heels, she had to be six feet tall. Her midnight hair was straight and fell freely over her shoulders in a black cascade.

A dramatic black-and-white dress left one tan shoulder bare. The slit in the straight skirt revealed long, shapely legs with each step. Her mother's Native American blood had given her smooth, olive skin, beautiful raven hair and her prominent cheekbones, yet she bore a striking resemblance to Will and reminded Garrett of Zach in her forthright, practical manner.

From the first moment she had captivated him. Dancing with her had fanned his desire until he ached to kiss her.

He shook his head to clear his thoughts.

While he hadn't lied to her, he had still deceived

her by not mentioning his ties to the Delaneys and his mission in Houston. At the moment she could be at her computer, looking him up and discovering he was an executive with Delaney Enterprises. A chill slithered through Garrett, turning him to ice. By breakfast time, she might already know the truth.

He didn't want her to find out that way. He wanted to tell her about his relationship with the Delaneys himself. But if he did, he wouldn't see her again, and neither the Delaneys nor she would get their inheritances.

His thoughts drifted to her soft, lush curves, her silky, midnight hair and her large, dark brown eyes...

After twenty more minutes of tossing and turning, he went to his indoor pool and swam laps, trying to stop thinking about Sophia yet wanting morning to come so he could see her again.

What if he did tell her about the Delaneys at breakfast? Maybe they already had enough of a connection that she'd agree to meet them.

Who was he kidding? Anyone who felt strongly enough to turn down billions wouldn't change her mind because of a few kisses and one exciting night.

Glumly, he executed a flip-turn and mulled it over as he swam another lap. Three billion dollars—no one could turn down money like that, yet she had. Why? Was her anger at Argus Delaney that deep?

From what the P.I. had unearthed, Argus had continued seeing her mother until she died. At the end of her life, he had done everything to keep her comfortable, taking care of her medical bills and seeing that she had the best care possible. Why was Sophia so bitter? She didn't seem a bitter, grudge-holding type. Sophisticated, intelligent, an inner core of steel, obviously hardworking, optimistic—all were qualities that he would use to describe her. It seemed difficult to imagine that she would have enough anger and hate to give up a three-billion-dollar inheritance.

He had to confess or risk Sophia discovering on her own the deception that grew larger with every passing hour.

Yet if he told her now, it was the end of what they'd only just started. And the termination of hope for the Delaneys.

Trying to shut off his nagging thoughts, he swore and swam harder.

It was another half hour before he was dry, sitting in his bedroom and staring out the window. Sleep eluded him. Worse, he was no closer to a decision about what he would do in a few hours when he saw her. Either way—tell her or wait—their relationship was doomed.

In spite of his disturbed sleep, the next morning he was eager to see Sophia again. His uncustomary inability to reach a decision about her added to his restlessness. Before he left to pick her up, Garrett phoned Will and gave him an update.

"Fantastic. So she can be civil and you like her," Will said. "That's promising."

"Will, for her to cut all of you off and lose her inheritance, her anger must run really deep. I can't imagine being able to persuade her to change her mind."

"We're counting on you to work a miracle. You're already getting close to her."

"Not that close," Garrett snapped and then curbed his impatience. "I wanted you to know that I'll be with her tonight so don't call."

"I'll wait until you call me. You're doing great—I knew you would."

"Will, stop being the ultimate optimist. She doesn't have a clue yet about my connections. Everything will change when she learns the truth."

"Maybe. Maybe not. Thank heavens women can't resist you."

Garrett had to laugh. "Oh, hell. Goodbye, Will. I'll call when I can."

Garrett ended the call and tried to get Will out of his thoughts and stop worrying about him. As he headed to his car, he focused on Sophia, his thoughts heating him to a torrid level.

When Sophia opened the door, her heart missed beats. Dressed in a charcoal suit and matching tie, Garrett looked as handsome as he had the night before.

His warm gaze roamed over her and he smiled. "You look gorgeous," he said.

"Thank you," she replied, thinking about all the different outfits she had tried on before settling on a plain red linen suit. Her hair was tied behind her head with a matching red scarf and he gave it a faint tug.

"Very pretty, but if we were going out for the evening, I would untie that scarf and let your hair free, which is the way I like it."

"But I won't," she replied lightly, locking up and walking to his car with him. "I have to go to the gallery and it needs to be tied and out of my way."

As he held the car door, she noticed he watched her legs when she climbed in. He closed the door and went around to slide behind the wheel. "So how did you sleep?" he asked.

"Great."

"I must be slipping if my kisses didn't keep you awake a little."

"You think I would tell you if I had stayed awake all night?"

As they both smiled, she felt the sparks between them, that electrifying current that had sizzled the whole time they were together last night. She hoped he never realized what a strong impact he had on her. She had a busy life and a time-consuming career. Garrett had come into her life at a time when she was trying to make a name in the art world. She didn't want him to realize how he affected her. She didn't want to lose control of her emotions.

At the restaurant, they were seated on an outdoor patio—the breezes were cool, the sun bright. As soon as they had ordered and were alone, Garrett smiled. "So when will my painting be delivered?"

"This afternoon."

"Excellent. Let me pick you up, we'll go to my house to hang the painting and then I'll take you out."

Her heartbeat quickened yet again. "You really don't waste time, do you," she replied.

"I'll pick you up around seven. So how much time do you spend in New Mexico?" he asked.

"Most of the summer. It's cool at night and I enjoy being there part of the year. Do you have a home anywhere else?"

"My home is in Dallas and I have a condo in Colorado because I like to ski. I also have a place in Switzerland."

"Nice."

"Painting is a reclusive occupation. Do you get out much in Santa Fe?"

"Sure, when I want to. But I enjoy the quiet and solitude. Chalk that up to being an only child." As Sophia talked, she couldn't help but study Garrett. His brown hair had been neatly combed, but the breeze soon shifted the locks and they tumbled over his forehead. His rough handsomeness—his hawk nose and firm jaw—and his spellbinding gray eyes fascinated her. When he began to speak, her gaze lowered to his mouth and she recalled his kisses, not hearing what he was saying as heat suffused her and the temperature of the cool morning changed.

He touched her chin with his fingers. "I don't believe you're hearing a word I'm saying. What could you possibly be thinking about?" he asked in a husky voice as if he guessed exactly why she hadn't heard a word he had said.

"My mind drifted, sorry," she said, embarrassed, looking into his knowing gaze. She felt the heat flush her cheeks and couldn't do anything to stop it.

"So, Sophia, where did it drift? What were you thinking?"

She gave up because he knew full well what she had been thinking about.

"I don't think you need me to tell you that, do you, Garrett?" He gave her a slight smile as she changed the subject. "Do you travel much with your job?"

To her relief he moved on with the conversation and the moment passed. But she suspected it had not been forgotten.

After breakfast Garrett took her to the gallery and parked beside her car. As he walked her to the door, he said, "We're early. May I come inside with you in case your building is empty?"

"Actually, people should start arriving in about ten minutes, and there is a guard outside."

"I'd rather stay until someone does arrive."

"Garrett, it's safe, and I'll lock the door once I'm inside." She turned to unlock the door and reached inside to switch off the alarm. When it became clear that he had no intention of leaving, she headed down the hall and said over her shoulder, "I'll show you my office."

She stepped into her office and he followed, taking in the beige room with bright splashes of color from her paintings. He studied the paintings for a moment, and then turned to her, making her pulse skip. "I expect people any minute now."

"I'll wait and be certain. Why don't you give me the key and I'll unlock the front and switch on lights."

She handed him the key and he caught her wrist, drawing her to him. Her "no" died on her lips before she ever uttered a sound. His arm banded her waist and he looked down at her. "I didn't sleep well and I suspect you didn't either. This is what I've wanted since I woke up this morning." His mouth covered hers, his lips warm and firm as he kissed her.

Her heart thudded while heat made the room a furnace. Wrapping her arm around his neck, she combed her fingers through his thick hair while their kiss turned to fire. Forgetting her surroundings, she held him tightly.

She never heard the car but Garrett raised his head and stepped away. "I hear one of your employees."

Garrett's erratic breathing matched hers. She felt disoriented, trying to ignore her desire and get her focus off Garrett and back to the real world.

He left to unlock the front for her just as she heard a car door slam. One of her male employees came in the back door, and Sophia introduced him to Garrett when he returned to the office.

"I'll pick you up at home tonight. How's six? Too early?" he asked.

"It's fine," she said, still slightly dazed, thinking six o'clock sounded eons away. "Thanks again for breakfast." He gave her an incredible smile, said goodbye and closed the door behind him. Sophia felt like she was in a daze until her phone rang.

"You were out late last night," Edgar said.

"Hello to you, too, Edgar," she said, amused. "I can't recall having a curfew. I don't think this is what Mom had in mind when she asked you to look out for me."

"I think it's exactly what she had in mind. You didn't answer the text I sent you this morning."

"Sorry, Edgar. I went out for breakfast."

"Uh-huh. With the Cantrell fellow?"

She laughed. "Yes, with the Cantrell fellow—Garrett, to be exact."

"Oh, dear," Edgar said, sighing audibly. "I suppose I will have to remember his name. So you're seeing him again?"

"Correct. Am I going to have to check in, Mom 2?"

He chuckled. "No. I'll keep tabs. Just answer your text messages."

"Yes, Edgar."

"Last night seemed a huge success."

"I'll hear shortly when everyone arrives at work."

"I'm certain I'm right. Have lunch with me and we'll celebrate your success."

"Thanks. That'll be nice." She made arrangements with him and a minute later, her assistant appeared to show her the receipts from the gallery.

Last night had indeed been a success—in more ways than one.

Sophia pulled on a blue wool-and-crepe sweater with a deep V-neck, a straight, short skirt and matching pumps. She put her hair up in a French twist. She was nervous, anxious, excited.

Get a grip, she silently lectured herself.

It wasn't easy. Garrett captivated her more than any other man she had known. He was exciting, handsome, interested in her life. If she let herself think of kissing him, she could get lost in memories of the previous night. But she didn't want that to happen. She needed to stay in control.

When she was ready, she studied herself thoroughly to make certain she was at her best for the evening.

When she opened the door to face him, her heart raced, despite all her commands to the contrary. In a navy suit, he looked breathtakingly handsome and commanding. His smile warmed her as his gaze drifted slowly over her.

"You're gorgeous," he said in a husky voice that was like a caress. She smiled, glad for the effort she had taken to get ready. "You have a nice home," he said.

"Sometime you'll get a tour, but right now, we're headed for your house."

"I'll hold you to that. Shall we go?"

Nodding, she closed the door behind her, hearing the lock click in place. Garrett took her arm to escort her to a waiting limo where the driver held the door while she climbed inside. She was surprised Garrett wasn't driving. Did he always travel in limos? Was she seeing another facet of his life? Garrett sat facing her.

"How were the gallery showings?"

"Very good. I'm gratified. I'll paint whether people buy my work or not, but when my paintings sell, I feel good about it. I keep the ones I don't want to sell. Some are just for me and they're not going to a gallery." As she talked, she was intensely aware of Garrett's smoky gaze on her. His fascinating gray eyes and knowledge of what his kisses could do kept her tingling with anticipation.

"If it suits you, we'll go out to my house to hang the painting. When we're through, we'll have dinner."

"Sounds like a great evening."

In a short time they drove through an exclusive residential area with acres of tall pines and estates set back out of sight. Black wrought-iron gates swung open to allow them entrance.

She was curious about his home, interested in finding out more about him. When the trees cleared, she saw the sprawling, three-story stone mansion.

"Garrett, your home is beautiful." A long narrow pool was centered in the formal gardens in the front yard. Various fountains held splashing water and sunlight spilled an orange glow over the house. Tall, symmetrical Italian pines stood at opposite ends of the wide porch that led to massive double doors.

The limo halted and the driver held the door as they exited. The door opened before they reached it and Garrett introduced her. "Sophia, meet Terrence, who is my right-hand man. He's butler and house manager and keeps things running smoothly here. Terrence, this is Ms. Rivers."

"Welcome, Ms. Rivers," Terrence said, stepping back and holding the door wide.

Garrett took her arm as they entered.

"Somehow this surprises me. I imagined you in a different type of home," she said, realizing Garrett had far more wealth than she had thought.

"Maybe I better not ask what kind."

"Something less formal, maybe more Western. Although this mansion has enough rooms to have all types of decor."

"I'll show you my shop and then we'll find the perfect spot for your painting."

He led her down the wide, elegant hall with potted palms and oils in ornate frames hanging on the walls. They entered another wing of the mansion and finally turned into a large paneled room that smelled of sawdust. The terrazzo floor was rust-colored with dark brown stones. Beautiful pieces of furniture in various stages were scattered throughout the room. The framework for an ornate credenza stood on a worktable, above which tools hung. One wall held handcrafted cabinets containing more tools.

She walked around the room, inhaling the sawdust smell, taking in the furniture in progress, lumber, power saws, a stack of sawhorses. "This is what you love, isn't it?"

He stood watching her and nodded. "You're the first woman who has ever been down here."

"I'm honored," she said.

"Sophia," he said and stopped. He stared at her intently.

"Yes?"

"I just wondered what you think about all this. Although I suppose I need to show you a finished product before I ask you that," he replied.

She had the feeling that he had been about to say something else, and she wondered what it was. The slight frown on his face made her curiosity deepen but she was certain if she asked, she would not get the answer.

She walked to a table to run her finger along the smooth finish. "This is beautiful, Garrett."

"That still needs a lot of work. It's intended to be a

reproduction of a French walnut refectory table. I also enjoy history."

"So do you do this when you can't sleep?" she asked.

"Do you paint when you can't sleep?" he said, by way of answering.

She smiled at him.

"C'mon. I'll show you some finished pieces."

As they made their way out into the hall, she still felt as if he towered over her—a unique sensation and one she enjoyed.

They paused by an elegant reproduction of a 19th-century French sofa with embroidered rosebuds in beige damask upholstery. "Here's a finished piece," he said.

She had expected his work to be nice, but this was beyond nice. "Garrett, this looks like a well-preserved antique. It looks like the real thing." She ran her fingers over the smooth wood. "This is truly beautiful," she said, impressed. "You could make another fortune from your craft."

He smiled. "That's the best compliment I've ever received," he said. He placed his hands on her shoulders. "You do look stunning, Sophia. Do you mind?" he said while he reached up and pulled a pin out of her hair. Locks spilled on her shoulders as she gazed up at him.

He stood close, removing pins, causing a gentle tingling sensation on her scalp. She looked at his mouth and her heart drummed. She wanted him to kiss her right now and was tempted to pull him to her.

Instead, she kept quiet while Garrett finished and her hair cascaded across her shoulders. She moved her head slightly, shaking out her hair and letting it swirl across her shoulders. She still watched him while he gazed into her eyes. His attention shifted to her mouth.

"Garrett, show me more of your work," she said, her

voice breathless. She wanted his kisses, yet she felt she should resist and have some control. Garrett had come into her life like a whirlwind and she needed to show some resistance before he totally uprooted her career and schedules. Deep down, she had an instinctive feeling that Garrett was more than just an appealing man who excited her.

"Better yet, come with me and I'll show you where I want to hang your painting. There are two possible rooms—one is the billiard room, the other is a large living area. I entertain there and it's not as formal as some of the other rooms."

She followed him down the wide hall. "You really need a map for this mansion."

He smiled. "Your place wasn't small either."

"I'm so accustomed to it, I don't give a thought to the size."

"Nor do I." He motioned toward open double doors. She entered a large room that had two glass walls. One end of the room bowed out in a sweeping glass curve, giving the room light and a sensation of being outdoors. The other end featured a massive brick fireplace. Leather furniture and dark fruitwood lent a masculine touch.

"This is a livable room. Very comfortable," he said. "I'm in here a lot." He led her across the room and she saw a familiar painting she had done a year earlier.

"I like it there," she said, looking at her painting on his wall with others in a grouping. "A prominent spot in a room you like and live in. Now you can think of me when you see it," she added lightly, teasing him.

"I'll always think of you when I see it," he said, his solemn tone giving a deeper meaning to his words.

"Sure you will," she said, laughing. "Is this the room where you'd like to hang the other painting?"

"Yes, possibly. Where do you think it should go?"

Aware of his attention on her, she strolled around the room, selecting and then rejecting spots until she stopped. "I think this is a good place."

"It is. One other possibility you should consider is over the hearth. It's a sizable painting. I think it fits this room."

"That would be the most prominent spot in the room," she said, surprised and pleased.

"I think it would look good there." He shed his coat. "Let me hold it up and see what you think."

She watched as he picked up the painting and held it in place.

She smiled at him. "It looks great there. Are you sure?"

He grinned. "I'll get tools and hang it."

"What can I do?" she asked.

"Let's have a drink and you can supervise the hanging."

"I can get the drinks," she said, moving to the bar in the corner of the room. "What would you like?"

"I think I'll have beer."

"And I'll have red wine," she stated. While she got a wineglass and opened a bottle, he disappeared. By the time he returned, she was on a leather couch in front of the fireplace with the drinks on a table. He placed an armload of tools on a chair and pulled off his tie. He twisted free the top buttons of his shirt—something so ordinary and simple yet it filled her with heat and she longed to get up and unbutton the rest for him. He picked up his beer, raising the bottle high.

"Here's to improving the looks of my house by adding a Sophia Rivers painting."

"I'll drink to that," she said, standing and picking up her drink to touch his cold bottle. Again, when she looked into his eyes, her heart skipped a beat. Each time they almost kissed, her longing intensified. How soon would they be in each other's arms?

Sipping her red wine, she stepped back. His gaze remained locked on hers. Watching her, he sipped his beer and then turned away, breaking the spell.

He picked up the painting. "I'll hold this and you tell me when I have it in exactly the right spot." He held the painting high, and then set it down. "Just a minute. I can put myself back together later," he said as he took off his gold cuff links and folded back his immaculate cuffs. "Now, let's try this again."

Slightly disheveled, he looked sexy, appealing. She tried to focus on the painting, but was having a difficult time keeping her attention off the man.

"To the right and slightly higher," she said. After several adjustments, she nodded. "That's perfect."

He leaned back to look while he held the picture. Setting it down, he picked up chalk to mark a place on the bricks before pulling the tape measure out.

She sipped her wine while he worked. In an amazingly short time he had her painting hanging in place and he stepped away.

"Let's look at it."

He took her arm and they walked across the large room to study the result of his work. She was aware of the warmth of him beside her. He looked at his watch. "Shall we go eat now, or should I just throw some steaks on the grill?"

"If we eat here, it's fine with me."

He leaned down to look directly into her eyes. "Are you certain you don't mind my cooking?"

"Now I'm curious," she said. "I'll view it as an adventure."

"Steaks at home it is." He draped his arm across her shoulders. "It's a nice evening. We'll eat on the terrace."

They carried their drinks outside, and Sophia was again surprised by the house.

"This isn't a terrace, Garrett—it's another kitchen, plus a terrace, plus a living area, plus a pool."

"With Houston's weather, it works well through the fall and winter," he replied, crossing to a stainless-steel gas grill built into a stone wall. In minutes he had the grill fired up and he sat with her on comfortable chairs in the outdoor living room.

"So where are you going, Sophia? What do you want out of life?"

"To pursue painting. To do charity work. I'd like to help with literacy. Also, try to do something to aid in getting more opportunities in school for children to take art and learn art appreciation. I want to open a gallery in New Mexico."

"Marriage and family?"

She shrugged. "I don't think about that. I'm accustomed to being on my own. I don't ever want to be in the situation my mother was in—in love with my dad who never returned that love fully."

"Your dad—you knew him?"

"What I told you last night wasn't completely accurate. He was around off and on all my life," she said, feeling a stab of pain and anger that had never left her. "My dad wouldn't marry my mother. He practically ignored me except for financial support."

"You said he was married?" Garrett said.

"Not by the time I was a teenager, but he didn't want to get tied down again. Whenever he came to visit, it tore her up each time he left. She would cry for several days. He was the only man she ever loved," Sophia stated bitterly. "He had a family—boys. He would go home to them. I couldn't do anything to help her or stop her tears. When I was little, we both cried. I cried for her and she cried over him."

"That's tough," Garrett said. "He ignored you?"

"In his way he provided for me. But looking back, I don't think he knew how to deal with a little girl. He brought me all kinds of presents. I can remember reaching an age where I smashed some of them to bits. Mom just started giving them to charities. I didn't want anything from him."

"How old were you then?"

"Probably about eight or nine. He was polite to me and Mom saw to it that I was polite to him, but we weren't together a whole lot. He never talked to me other than hello and goodbye. I rarely heard him say my name. When I was little I wondered whether he knew it. Often, I would be sent to my grandmother's, which I loved, or out with my nanny when he was coming. Worked fine for me. I didn't want to see him."

"Yet your mother always loved him."

"She did. And I don't ever want to fall into that trap. The best way to avoid it is to keep relationships from becoming too deep."

"Maybe you shouldn't base everything on the actions of your father."

"That's the legacy he left me—a deep fear of any relationship that isn't totally committed."

"Sorry, Sophia," Garrett said with a somber note.

"How'd we get on this?" she asked, wanting to avoid

thinking and talking about her blood father. She wanted him out of her life and thoughts as much as humanly possible.

"I'm interested in your life and finding out about you. Did he ever try to make it up to you?"

She thought of the inheritance Argus Delaney had left her. "He always showered Mom with money. Money was his solution for everything. He paid her medical bills, but by the time the end of her life came, we had enough money to manage on our own. No matter what happened, she always loved him. And I've always hated him," she said.

"At least he was good to her," Garrett said gently. "And generous."

"I suppose I should be grateful, but I can't be. He left money when he died—money I don't want one penny of," she said.

"He's gone. He'll never know whether you take his money or refuse it. Why not take it and enjoy it? It should be yours."

She shook her head, feeling the familiar current of fury that she had lived with as long as she could remember.

"I don't want anything to do with him."

"You could do a lot with your inheritance."

"I'll never touch it," she said, trying to shift her focus off the past and onto Garrett, thinking he would be fascinating to paint. His rugged features gave him a distinctive individualism and his unique gray eyes were unforgettable. Desire stirred and once again, she struggled to pay attention to their conversation.

He was studying her intently. "Sophia—" He paused, his eyes holding secrets. She couldn't tell what he was thinking.

"What? What were you going to say?"

He looked away. "I'll check on the steaks." She watched him stride to the cooker and she wondered for the second time this evening what it was he'd been about to say to her. Probably more advice about taking her inheritance, which she'd already heard enough of from Edgar.

"The steaks are ready."

She stood, going with him to help get tossed salads, potatoes and water on the table. Soon they sat on the terrace to eat thick, juicy steaks.

"It's a wonder you ever travel for pleasure. It's gorgeous here and you have every convenience."

"I like it here, but I like my other places, too."

"I guess I can understand since I enjoy Santa Fe and Taos and even the cabin in the mountains as much as living in Houston." She took a bite of her steak. "You're a very good cook. The steak is delicious," she said, surprised because he'd seemed to pay little attention to his cooking.

"I'm glad you think so."

"I should have watched you more closely. I invariably burn them."

"You can watch me as closely as you want," he replied with a twinkle.

"I opened the door for that one," she said, smiling at him. "So how did you get into property management?" she asked, picking up her water glass to take a sip. A faint breeze caught his hair, blowing it gently. His hair was thick, and she thought about how it felt to run her fingers through it.

"My dad had the business," he was saying. "He was into property management and finance. I was raised to follow in his footsteps and groomed to take over his businesses."

"Businesses? There are others?"

"Yes, but I'm not directly involved in most of them. Hardly involved at all. They're investments."

"And that leaves you free to play around," she said. "So what do you actually do?" she asked, flirting with him while trying to satisfy her curiosity about him and his life.

He smiled at her. "More than play around, although I hope to do that tonight. Dinner—get to know you—kiss you. That's what I want to do in the next few hours," he said, his voice deepening and making her tingle.

"I don't really know you. Do you work, Garrett, or does the playboy lifestyle fit you?"

"I work, but not tonight, so we can get away from that subject. You aren't eating, and I've lost my appetite for this steak. Let's sit where it's more comfortable to talk. We can take our drinks with us."

She was leaving a half-eaten steak, yet she couldn't resist his suggestion. Her interest in food had disappeared with Garrett's flirting. He took her hand and she stood, going with him, her insides tingling the moment he touched her.

Garrett sat close on the couch. Her perfume was an exotic fragrance and he liked the faint scent. Her long hair was silky in his fingers as he twisted and toyed with the strands. She was stunning and he couldn't get enough of her. And yet, he was racked with guilt.

When she had talked about Argus Delaney, Garrett felt awful that he wasn't telling her the truth about who he was. Twice he had been on the verge, almost confessing and then pausing, waiting because it seemed the wisest course to follow. If he confessed the truth now, he was certain he would be finished. It was too soon, but knowing that didn't ease his conscience.

"What about you and marriage?" she asked.

"I'm a workaholic, I suppose," he said, stretching out his long legs. "I haven't ever been deeply in love," he admitted. "I don't feel ready for marriage or getting tied down. Right now, my life is devoted to my work."

"Pretty ordinary attitude when someone is tied up in work," she stated.

As he gazed into her eyes, he wondered what it would be like to come home to her every night—to make love to her night and day. His thoughts surprised him. Sophia stirred him in a way no woman before her ever had. He had never had long-term thoughts or speculation about a woman before. Not even when he had been in a relationship. "I owe you an elegant dinner and dancing instead of sitting at my house and eating my cooking and helping me hang your painting," he said, trying to get focused again on the present and stop imagining a future with her. That kind of thinking disturbed him. Because it was totally uncustomary.

"I'm enjoying the evening. You don't owe me an elegant dinner," she said. "This has been nice and you're an interesting man, Garrett Cantrell."

Garrett smiled at her. "You barely know me. And I lead an ordinary life."

"Why do I doubt that statement? You've bought two of my paintings. That alone makes you interesting."

"Next time we go to your house and I get to see where you paint," he said.

"It's a typical studio with brushes and paint smears. I don't think it's quite as interesting as your workshop."

"If it's yours, it's interesting. Have you painted all your life?"

"Actually, yes. I loved drawing and painting. Of course, what little girl doesn't?"

As she talked about painting when she was a child, his mind returned to the problem. He hated not telling her about the Delaneys, yet he had heard the bitterness, felt her anger smoldering. He wanted to be up front with her—his guilt was deepening by the minute.

He realized she was staring at him with a quizzical smile. "What?" he asked.

"You haven't heard one word I've been saying, Garrett. Is there something you want to tell me? What are you thinking about?"

He focused on her lips before looking into her eyes again while desire consumed him. He didn't want to admit the truth yet and the burden of guilt was becoming unbearable, but one way to avoid both was to stop her questions with kisses.

Three

Sophia gazed at Garrett, waiting for an answer to her question, wondering what he had on his mind. Was it his business that had him so lost in his own thoughts?

Was it her?

"Garrett, what is it?" she asked, looking into his eyes.

Lust was blatant, causing her pulse to race. Perhaps it *was* her.

He leaned close, slipping his arm around her waist to pull her to him, ending her questions as his mouth covered hers. Her heart slammed against her ribs.

She inhaled, winding her arms around his neck while she kissed him in return. When he pulled her onto his lap, she was barely aware of moving.

He wound his fingers in her hair and she clung to him. Her body tingled, an aching need beginning. She moaned softly as he ran his hand down her back, over the curve of her hip to her thighs. He pushed the hem of her skirt higher to touch her bare skin. Hot, urgent longing consumed her. Her fingers worked free the remaining buttons of his shirt and she pushed it away to touch his sculpted chest. She ran her fingers lower over his muscled stomach. The touch caused the fires within her to blaze. She gasped over caressing him, realizing she had to stop or she would be lost in lovemaking, complicating her life in a manner she had always intended to avoid. She had never slept with a man and she didn't intend to take that step now.

She caught his wrist and raised her head. "This is crazy, Garrett. I barely know you. We're going too fast."

"We're getting to know each other, and I'd say the chemistry is pretty hot." As he talked, he ran both hands through her hair on either side of her face. "You're beautiful. You take my breath away. Sophia, I want to make love to you," he whispered hoarsely.

Her heart thudded but she forced herself to slide off his lap. "Let's take a breather and slow things down," she said, standing to face him.

He stood, his desire obvious. His shirt was unbuttoned to the waist and pushed open to reveal his broad, muscled, masculine chest. Her mouth was dry and she had to fight the urge to fling her arms around his neck and kiss him again.

"I haven't felt this way about anyone before," he said, sounding surprised, frowning slightly as if he weren't happy about it.

"Please sit, Sophia. We'll just talk," he said.

She sat, turning so she could face him. The moment he was seated, he wrapped his fingers in her hair. "We can sit and talk, but I can't keep from touching you."

"Garrett, I meant it when I said I'm not into affairs.

I watched my mother shed a million tears over my father. I won't put myself in that position."

"I can understand that completely. But we're not having an affair. We're kissing."

"I know. But things are escalating quickly," she said.

"Well, now I'm duly warned about your feelings," he said with a smile.

"I figure it's better to be forthright and upfront with you. Why are you smiling?"

"I didn't mean to. You just remind me of a friend who is forthright," he replied, combing his fingers slowly through her hair, caressing her nape and then picking up long strands to wind them in his fingers again. "Sophia, I already feel as if I've known you a long time."

"I like that," she said, trying to focus on their conversation, yet more aware of his hand lightly toying with her hair.

"So. Let's talk. Do you have other relatives?" he asked. "Did your mother have any brothers or sisters?"

"I have two aunts, one uncle and eight cousins, all scattered around this part of Texas. I see them at family events, but otherwise, we haven't been that close since she's been gone. I never knew my father's family, nor did I want to," she said coldly.

"You might be making a mistake there," Garrett said.

Sophia felt her blood turn to ice, and she glared at Garrett. "No, I'm not. His family was the reason he wouldn't marry my mother. I don't want to know them or have anything to do with any part of him."

"Sophia, *you're* part of him. And they couldn't help being part of him any more than you could."

She hadn't ever thought about how innocent they were of what their father did, and the thought startled her, but she pushed it away. His sons were still his blood.

"Even so, they grew up with him. They have his name and he's honored them." Why did Garrett keep taking Argus's side? She disliked talking about her father or even thinking about him. "Garrett, let's find something else to discuss. Do you have any other hobbies besides the furniture?"

"Sure. I work out. I ski. I play tennis, play polo and I swim. You?"

"More things we have in common. I love rodeos, country dances. I also like to ski, swim and I play the piano," she answered.

"With the storms that have gone through recently, they've already had enough freezing weather in the upper levels of Colorado mountains to ski. Fly up there with me for the weekend. We can leave early in the morning and come back Sunday evening."

"You're serious," she said, surprised by his invitation.

"Why not? We'll have fun, ski, nothing big. Just a fun getaway. My condo is large. You can take your pick of bedrooms."

"You are serious." A weekend with Garrett. Excitement bubbled and she wanted to accept, yet common sense reminded her again to slow down with him. He had come into her life like a whirlwind.

He leaned closer and held her chin. "Come with me. No strings. I'll bring you home anytime you want. We'll ski, relax, talk. Do whatever we want."

Her heartbeat quickened. She was surprised at herself because his offer held some appeal. On the other hand, years of being wary of getting too close to someone were ingrained in her.

"I don't think flying to Colorado with you is a good idea."

"Sophia, you're not going to risk getting hurt by spending the weekend skiing with me. We're not getting into anything remotely serious."

"But this is exactly how you get into something serious. Moment after moment together and then it's too late."

"Take a risk and live a little. This is simply two days. We're not going to fall in love over the weekend."

She blushed. She hadn't been worried about falling in love.

Had she?

"If you're worried, we can ask Edgar to join us."

She couldn't keep from laughing. "You're willing to invite Edgar, too?"

"If that's what it takes to spend the weekend with you, yes, I'll invite Edgar, too."

"Now you're making me feel foolish."

"That's not my intention. Listen, I understand why you don't want to follow in your mother's footsteps, but I don't think you run any risk of that happening with me."

Her eyes widened. "I guess I've lumped all males into the same group as my father."

"I can't blame you for being hurt, Sophia," he said solemnly and her heart warmed. He gazed intently at her while she debated, waiting quietly.

"I'll go with you," she said, smiling at him.

"Excellent. It'll be fun. No big deal."

It was a big deal because she didn't even spend weekends with men she knew. All she had to go on with Garrett was the information she had received about him from others and her own feelings.

"I'll tell Edgar I'm going, but we're not inviting him along. He hates cold weather and he can't imagine fastening his feet to 'long boards,' as he calls them. Thank you, though, for the offer to invite him," she said.

"Good. I'll check the weather right now. I don't fly into storms if I can possibly avoid it."

She watched as he pulled out his phone. He smiled broadly, sexy creases bracketing his mouth. "Good weather—cold nights, sunny days. I'll call my pilot. How early can we go?"

"Name your time."

"I'll pick you up at seven."

"Fine with me," she said. She'd surprised herself, she thought as eagerness bubbled in a steady current. The weekend with Garrett. Foolhardy, risky for her heart.

Exciting.

Walking away, Garrett talked with the pilot and made arrangements. When he was done, he sat beside her again. "We're set to fly at eight."

"So one of your traits is impulsiveness," she said. "I'm learning more about you."

"I don't think I'd describe myself as impulsive. Usually I'm predictable and methodical."

"If we get to know each other, I'll weigh in on that."

"We'll get to know each other, Sophia," he said softly in a husky tone that sent a tingle spiraling in her. "I definitely intend that we do."

Desire was constant with Garrett, keeping her intensely aware of him in a physical manner. Despite her concerns, she couldn't deny that she loved being with him, hearing about him, learning about him. In some ways, she, too, felt as if she had known him a long time. They talked until one and she promised herself by half past she would end the evening. Finally, when it was almost two, she stood.

"Garrett, I must get home."

"You don't have to go if you don't want." He waved his hand toward his house. "Needless to say, there is plenty of room here. Take any bedroom you want. Close to mine, far from mine or in mine with me," he teased. "I'll even promise to not wake you in the morning. Particularly if you make the last choice."

Shaking her head, she laughed. "It does seem silly for you to drive me home, but that's what I want. If I'm going to Colorado to ski, I want to go home and get some things."

"All right. Home it is. I told my chauffeur we'd take you home tonight."

"See, I should have driven."

"I would insist on taking you home even if you had driven. It's way too late for you to be out driving around by yourself."

"That's an old-fashioned notion."

"It's not the first time someone has accused me of having old-fashioned notions."

"I think old-fashioned is rather nice if it isn't overdone. Edgar gets a little carried away— I'll probably have a text waiting from him when I get in. He's probably running background checks on you as we speak."

She expected a laugh but Garrett merely gave her a smile and stood. "Shall we go?"

When they arrived at her house, the limo waited while Garrett walked with her to her door. He stepped inside, waiting while she switched off the alarm and then pulling her into his embrace to kiss her.

With her heart racing, she wrapped her arms around him and kissed him in return, pouring her feelings into her kiss, wanting to spend the rest of the night with him, wanting to touch and caress and make love, yet knowing she should do little more than what they were doing unless she wanted to risk losing her heart.

How much time passed, she didn't know or care. They were breathless, wanting more. Need became a raging fire. When Garrett's hands began to roam over her, she stopped him and stepped back.

"We'll say good-night," she stated. Her voice was breathless as she gulped for air. "Garrett, tonight has been so much fun," she said softly. His gray eyes had darkened to slate, desire burning in their depths. "Thanks for a grand evening."

"I'll see you in the morning, Sophia," he said, giving her a smile that nearly stopped her heart. He turned and left, the lock clicking in place behind him.

For a moment, she could barely move, resting against the door, trying desperately to catch her breath, wondering if she was about to make the biggest mistake of her life.

Garrett swore under his breath. He liked Sophia more than any woman he had known. He wanted to call Will immediately and tell him that he hated deceiving her and it had to end. But he knew that as soon as he told Sophia the Delaneys had sent him, she would break it off.

He was torn between admitting the truth to her and running the risk of losing her, or continuing the deception until he felt she liked him enough that they could weather the storm that would break when he told her the truth.

More than once he had mulled over resigning from Delaney Enterprises and devoting himself to building furniture. Sometimes he thought of working with his hands, living in a place near the ocean, creating instead of acquiring. He often wondered if the notion of changing careers was merely a pipe dream, yet Sophia had successfully done just that.

Only her situation had been different. He had been raised to do this kind of work and he felt he owed the Delaney family his services. Argus Delaney had taken his father out of poverty, given him a job and paid for his education because he said he saw potential in his dad. His father had worked hard and risen fast and Argus had helped him all along the way, opening doors and paying him well. In turn, his father had absolute loyalty to the Delaneys and had raised Garrett to feel the same. If he left Delaney Enterprises, Garrett felt he would be turning his back on all his father had wanted for him, and on Will's friendship. And he was inheriting a fortune from Will's dad.

Even so, the thought was tempting. Especially after being with Sophia.

For the first time he considered actually going through with telling Will he was resigning. If he resigned, he might have hope of some kind of future with Sophia.

How tempting. He could tell Sophia everything with a clear conscience.

Could he do it?

At his estate he glanced at his watch and picked up his phone to call Will. "Sorry for the early hour."

"I hope it's because you have good news."

"I don't, and I don't know whether I ever will. She told me more about your dad. She's incredibly bitter."

"Are you making any progress?"

"We're flying to Colorado to ski for the weekend."

"I call that progress. Just hang in there—sounds as

if you two get along fine," Will said, his voice rising with enthusiasm.

"We do," Garrett said in clipped tones. "I don't know what will happen when I tell her the truth. Will, I hate not being up front with her on this."

"You're doing her a favor, too—don't forget that."

"Dammit, Will, she's been hurt. She isn't going to change easily and I can't keep up this deception," Garrett said, startled by how deeply concerned he had become over Sophia's feelings. He cared more for her than he would have dreamed possible when he first took this assignment.

"You don't need to feel guilty. You're doing your job. Do your best is all we all ask—your best is mighty damn fine. We're counting on you."

"I know. I'll see how it goes today."

"Don't rush. Get her so close she'll do what you want."

Garrett hated the sound of that. "I'll talk to you tomorrow or Monday," he said.

"Have a real good time."

He hung up, wondering why he'd even bothered to call Will. He stared at the phone with Will's words echoing in his thoughts. *We're counting on you.* All his adult life they had counted on him. He couldn't toss that aside.

Doubting if he would sleep at all, he skipped bed and headed to the shower, thinking of being with her again, of her dark eyes and midnight hair, her laughter, her kiss. A whole weekend. By the time they flew back to Texas, he hoped to be closer to her.

The big question was: What would happen if he told her the truth? Would he lose her forever?

* * *

Sophia rummaged in her closet for ski clothes and other things she would need. Still marveling at the thought that she had accepted Garrett's offer, she decided to wait to text Edgar until the morning.

Anticipation kept a running current of excitement humming through her body. She kept glancing at the clock, anxious to see Garrett again. Was she falling into the same trap her mother had fallen into? Was she doing what she had tried all her adult life to avoid— falling in love?

A text message broke into her thoughts.

Are you home? I've been worried about you. All OK?

She fired back an answer.

I'm home, Edgar. Flying to Colorado tomorrow to ski with Garrett. Back Sunday. Don't worry about me. Go to bed.

Minutes after she sent the text, her phone rang. "Edgar, do you know what time it is?"

"I know you're still awake," he answered. "I hope you keep in touch. Sophia, this isn't like you. How important is Garrett Cantrell to you?"

"I like the guy and we're becoming friends. I can do that," she said, hoping she could hold true to her words. "We'll be back home early Sunday evening."

"I just want to keep my promise to your mother."

"Stop worrying. Mom had no idea you would take her request to this extent. I'm grown, Edgar. I can take care of myself."

"All right, I'll buzz off. Let me know when you're back in town. You can tell me all about your weekend."

Smiling, she put away her phone and climbed into bed.

Just a few short hours later, Garrett was at her door. As he stepped inside, his gaze roamed over her.

She smiled while her heart jumped. Each time they were together, she thought he was more handsome than the time before. Dressed in a cable-knit navy sweater and jeans, he took her breath away.

"You look gorgeous," he said, wrapping one arm around her waist and leaning down to kiss her. She wound her arms around his neck to kiss him in return.

With an effort she moved away. "This is not a weekend for seduction," she said with a smile.

"That's simply a good morning kiss," he said. "And I know what I promised you. We'll keep things light. Unless you change your mind," he added with a grin. "The weather report is good so we're on our way." He picked up her skis, shouldering her bag as she gathered her purse and jacket.

"Sorry, the tour of my house will have to wait," she said.

"Something to look forward to in the coming week. Perhaps Monday night."

She laughed at his attempt to make plans with her for Monday even though they hadn't even gone away for the weekend yet.

At the airport, they boarded a waiting jet that was far larger than she had expected. Its luxurious interior made her forget she was on board a plane for a few moments.

As they flew, Garrett sat facing her, their knees almost touching. It was difficult to keep her mind on the conversation because she was lost in looking at him. She still marveled at her reaction to him, alternating between enjoying it and being concerned by it. *Remember, it's just a fun weekend,* she told herself.

Far sooner than she expected they were driving through the small Colorado resort town to Garrett's condo.

His condo was built of stone with panoramic mountain views. Polished plank floors gleamed beneath high, open-beamed ceilings. Garrett built a roaring fire in the massive stone fireplace.

"What a change this is. It's a picture book," she said, looking out the window that covered almost the entire front wall.

Garrett stood behind her with his arms lightly around her. "We can hit the slopes or wait, if you prefer."

"We came to ski. I vote to ski."

"All right. I'll meet you back here in twenty minutes."

She went to the bedroom she had selected on the opposite end of the hall from Garrett's, which had made him smile. She changed into her gear, finally gathering her parka, sunglasses and gloves. They spent the rest of the day on the slopes, discovering they were well-matched skiers. They returned as the sun was setting.

"When we're changed, I'll take you to my favorite restaurant," Garrett said, stomping snow off his feet inside the entryway.

"Sounds good to me—I'm starving."

"Meet you here in, what?"

"Give me thirty minutes," she replied.

Certain he would be ready in far less time, she hurried. Thirty minutes later she made one last check. Her red wool pants and sweater were warm, as were her fur-lined boots. She let her hair go unpinned. With a toss of her head to get her long hair away from her face, she went to meet him.

As she entered the room, only one small lamp burned

and she could see the view of the sparkling lights through the picture window. The view was spectacular with twinkling lights below spreading out toward the snow-covered mountains that glistened beneath a rising full moon. But when Garrett entered the room, she only had eyes for him. He wore a bulky sweater that emphasized his broad shoulders, tight jeans and Western boots. He stepped closer and his direct gaze held her. Desire shone in the smoky depths of his eyes.

"Now this is best of all," he said. "You look beautiful. I love your hair down." He wrapped his fingers in her hair and his arm circled her waist as he pulled her close. "This is perfect," he whispered before he covered her mouth with his.

Ending their kiss, she tried to catch her breath, noticing that his breathing was as ragged as hers. Taking his cue from her, he stepped back.

"Shall we go?" he said in a husky voice while he caressed her nape.

He held her parka and she pulled on her gloves as they went downstairs to the car. During the ride she looked at the charming snow-covered town, but her thoughts tumbled over the excitement of being here with Garrett and the worry of how important he was becoming in her life.

At the restaurant they sat close to a blazing fire while piano music played softly. They ordered cups of steaming cider and hors d'oeuvres. Garrett had been famished when he finished dressing, but now his appetite had dwindled. He longed to hold Sophia, to kiss her. He ached to just touch her, to physically keep contact. Her hair fell loosely over her shoulders and around her face. Her luminous brown eyes were thickly lashed and captivating. And she looked happy.

Which made what he had to do even harder.

This withholding of information had gone on long enough. The closer they got, the more important it was to be honest with her. He had never been devious in his dealings before and he didn't want to start now.

It was a miracle she hadn't already discovered his connection with the Delaneys. But he was certain he would know when she had.

How he wished he didn't have this big secret. If only he were free to pursue her honestly the way he wanted, in a manner he had never dreamed of before.

Candlelight on the table reflected in her dark eyes. Each day he had been amazed by how much he wanted to be with her. She was becoming more important to him by the minute. Which meant he needed to tell her.

"You're an excellent skier," she said.

"I was going to tell you the same."

She smiled. "I think you held back to stay with me. It was invigorating, a real change from my regular life. You've turned my world topsy-turvy."

And there it was—the perfect opening to tell her about the Delaneys.

But he couldn't. He realized he didn't want to tell her in public. He wanted to be alone with her. And he also realized that no matter how guilty he was feeling, he should wait until they returned to Houston. It would give him the weekend to get closer to her and hopefully create a stronger bond between them that would be harder for her to break.

A voice inside him told him that that was a cruel thing to do, but he ignored it.

He didn't want to lose her. From the first moment he

had seen her, he'd been drawn to her and the thought of losing her made his insides churn. He had never expected to find her fascinating, to want a relationship with her.

"Maybe you've turned mine topsy-turvy, too."

"I seriously doubt that," she said. "All of this is scrumptious," she added, taking a bite of a mini-beef Wellington. I can see why this is your favorite restaurant."

"Good—I'm so glad you like it. So tell me, do you go to your gallery every day?"

"Not at all. I have a competent manager and excellent staff. They run the business so I can stay at the studio and paint."

"I don't blame you. If I ever build furniture full-time, I'll do the same."

"Why do you stay in property management? With your talent for woodwork, you could build a following very quickly."

"Blame my father for that one. I was raised to be in a productive, lucrative business. It was instilled in me as far back as I can remember."

"But your father is gone now, and you've already proved yourself in that area. Your furniture would be productive and lucrative."

"I'm wound up in obligations. Imagined or real, they are as much a part of me as my breathing. To Dad, who hasn't been gone that long, my fascination with building was entertainment and silly."

"Too bad," she said, shaking her head. "What did your dad want for you in your personal life?"

"The usual. Marriage and kids. But I've watched too many people have miserable marriages, and I'm not ready to get tied down."

"Tied down," she repeated, smiling. "So no long relationships in your past?"

"None. And evidently, none in yours."

"Absolutely not."

When he had first met her, her answer would have pleased him—a woman who did not want any deep commitment. Why now did he feel jolted slightly by her answer? Was Sophia weaving a web around his heart—something no woman had ever done?

It was nine before they left the restaurant. When they stepped outside a light snow fell, big flakes drifting, glistening in the light.

"Look, Garrett, this is enchanting," she said, spinning around with her arms spread wide. Her long hair flew out behind her, swirling around her face. He couldn't resist wrapping his arms around her to kiss her, tasting a wet snowflake on her lips.

When he released her, she stepped away. "We're in public."

"I couldn't resist," he admitted, thinking he would always remember her spinning around in the snow, a beautiful woman whose exuberance and zest for life were contagious. He looked up at the falling flakes and took out his phone. "We weren't supposed to have this kind of weather."

"It's gorgeous. I can't keep from being glad we have it."

"Even if you're snowbound with me?" he asked.

"Even if. I'll manage."

"Chance of a trace of snow," he read off his phone. "Clear Sunday." On impulse he glanced up. "Do it again. Let me get your picture."

Laughing but humoring him, she did and he took a picture that he expected to be a blur, a disappointment.

Instead, the picture was clear with her dark hair swinging out behind her head. He had caught her big smile and the essence of the moment. It would have been a perfect moment if it weren't for this big secret between them. He put away his phone, shaking off the thought. "A trace of snow tonight won't make any difference except to please you."

"It definitely does," she said. "Hey, wait. You're not the only one who wants a picture of this." She yanked out her phone. "Smile, Garrett."

He grinned while she took his picture and then flashed it briefly so he had a glimpse of himself. Linking his arm in hers, he waited for the valet to bring his car.

They stomped snow off their boots at his condo and he built another fire, which gave a low light. When he turned away from the hearth, he faced her.

Sophia stood at the window with the flickering orange flames playing over her. As his gaze drifted down over her lush curves and long legs, his heartbeat quickened. His longing was intense. He crossed the short distance to take her in his arms.

Four

Sophia's heart thudded as she wrapped her arms around Garrett. The day had been magical and she had grown closer to him, learning more about him and enjoying herself. All through dinner she had wanted to be alone with him so they could be together like this again.

Snowflakes had been the perfect touch, landing in his dark hair, sprinkling across his broad shoulders. His kiss had tantalized her. She wanted more of him, so much more.

She didn't believe in love at first sight, or second or third for that matter. She thought if she ever fell in love it would be with someone she had been friends with for years, yet Garrett shook her theories because he was already more important to her than anyone else she had ever dated. He was pure temptation.

He made her want to risk her heart.

She stood on tiptoe, her heart pounding while he

held her tightly against his long frame. His hand slid down her back and up beneath her sweater. She moaned softly, the sound muffled by his mouth on hers. His fingers trailed up her back in a feathery touch that was electrifying.

He picked her up and carried her closer to the fire, setting her on her feet while he still kissed her as flames crackled. Garrett stepped back and pulled her sweater over her head, tossing it aside. He unfastened her lacy bra and removed it, dropping it to the floor.

With a deep sigh he stepped back, cupping her breasts in his hands. "So beautiful," he said, his gaze as sensual as his caresses. His thumb traced circles on her nipples that sent currents streaming from his touch.

She tugged his sweater over his head to toss it aside. She moaned in pleasure again while her hands roamed over his broad, muscled chest, her fingers tangling in a thick mat of chest hair that tapered to a narrow line disappearing beneath his belt.

Firelight spilled over him, highlighting bulging muscles, leaving dark shadows on flat planes. His handsome features captivated her, and in some ways she felt as if she had known him for years instead of days, just as he had said to her.

Desire wracked her. She wanted to make love. She ran her hands over his flat stomach until he leaned down to kiss each breast, his tongue tracing circles. She gasped again with pleasure, closing her eyes and clinging to him while fire raged within her.

She wanted him with an urgency she had never felt before. Garrett was special, unique in her life and she didn't think Garrett would ever hurt her. It was a night, not a relationship. Was she succumbing in the same foolish way to temptation, just as her mother had done in allowing a man to become irresistible?

All her logic fled, driven away by passion when his arm banded her waist again, pulling her tightly against him. He picked her up again to carry her to a sofa, settling her on his lap. Her bare breasts were pressed against his warm chest, the thick mat of chest hair sensual against her naked skin. As they kissed his hands roamed over her, light caresses that scalded.

Kisses became hotter, deeper and more passionate and she didn't notice his hands at the buttons on her pants. He pushed them down, standing and setting her on her feet to let them fall around her ankles.

He paused, stepping back to lift one of her feet to remove her boot and sock and then he moved to the other foot, standing to hold her hips while his gaze drifted slowly over her. "You're lovely, so beautiful," he whispered. He yanked off his boots and socks, tossing them aside. When he stood, she unfastened his belt and pulled it free, dropping it and unbuttoning his jeans to push them off. As he kicked them away, he pulled her into his arms.

This was the time to stop if she was going to, but she had already made a decision that went against everything she had practiced. Take a chance with Garrett tonight. Tomorrow she could say no. She had never had a weekend like this one and might not ever again. She gazed into his gray eyes that were heavy-lidded, filled with sensual promises. She wanted him to an extent she had never wanted any man. She wanted to be loved by Garrett. She could take what she wanted, and then go back to her resolutions and her safe life.

Garrett drove all thoughts away with his kisses and caresses.

Her insides knotted, fires building low in her. He sat and pulled her onto his lap against his thick rod, caressing her while one hand dallied lightly along her legs, moving to the inside of her thighs, heightening desire.

Continuing to kiss her, he leaned over her while his fingers went beneath the flimsy bikini panties. She spread her legs slightly, giving him more access, moaning with pleasure and need.

He touched her intimately, kissing her, his other hand caressing her breast while his fingers were between her legs. Pleasurable torment built as he stood again to peel away her panties.

Freeing him, she removed his briefs, caressing his hard manhood, stroking and then kissing him. He closed his eyes, his hands winding in her hair while he groaned. In seconds, he raised her up, looking into her eyes.

He picked her up once again, carrying her to the bedroom, placing her on the bed and then shifting to her ankle to kiss her, trailing kisses along her leg to the back of her knee. Gradually, his tongue moved up the inside of her thigh. Writhing, she closed her eyes while he moved between her legs, driving her wild with his tongue and fingers.

She sat up swiftly, wrapping her arms around him and pulling him down. He held her tightly, kissing her fervently.

"Garrett, I don't have any protection," she whispered.

"I do," he answered. He left, and in seconds returned with a small packet, which he opened. He spread her legs and knelt between them to put on the condom and then he lowered himself.

He started to enter her and she wrapped her legs around him. As he lowered himself and thrust slowly, he stopped. "Sophia," he said, frowning and sounding shocked.

She held him tightly. "I know what I want," she whispered.

"You're a virgin," he said, starting to pull away.

"Garrett," she whispered, holding on to keep him from leaving. "Love me," she whispered. "I want you to," she said before kissing him passionately. He hesitated a moment and then slowly pushed into her, sending a sharp pain that was gone when he filled her and slowly moved in her.

In seconds she rocked with him, lost in desire. The tension increased. Garrett was covered in sweat, moving with her, trying to pleasure her while urgency grew. And then all control was gone. He pumped fast and she met him, clinging to him as relief burst and rapture poured over her.

"Garrett," she cried out, holding him tightly, spinning away in ecstasy, oblivious of all else.

He shuddered with his release and then showered kisses on her, slowing as his ragged breathing calmed.

They were finally still, wrapped together, her heartbeat returning to normal. She held him tightly while her fingers played over one muscled shoulder.

"You should have told me," he said.

"It didn't matter."

"Yes, it did. I tried to avoid hurting you."

She framed his face with her hands and kissed him lightly. "You couldn't hurt me," she said and saw something flicker in the depths of his eyes that was like a warning bell to her, yet had it been her imagination? The warmth in his eyes now enveloped her and she pushed away her worry.

He rolled over, keeping her with him, their legs entangled. He combed long strands of hair away from her face and smiled at her. "You're beautiful," he whispered, kissing her lightly.

"Garrett, when I flew up here, I was certain this would never happen," she said, running her fingers over his bare shoulder.

He showered light kisses on her temple down to her ear. "I actually hadn't planned on it either. I didn't think you'd want to make love." He propped himself up on an elbow to look down at her, gazing intently. "I'll never hurt you, Sophia. I'll never be like your father."

"Shh, Garrett. Let me enjoy the moment now," she said lightly, touched by his statement. She noticed his voice had deepened, his words sounding heartfelt. She combed his brown hair back from his forehead. "This was a one-time thing. I'll go right back to my former resolutions because that's the safe way to live and protect my heart," she said.

He kissed the corner of her mouth lightly. "We'll see what the future brings," he whispered, placing more kisses on her throat.

She ran her fingers along his jaw. "This was perfect. I'll always remember it."

"I agree with that. Monday night I want to see your house, particularly your studio."

"That's a deal. But I think you'll be disappointed. My studio is just an art studio with all the mess that goes with painting."

"It'll be fascinating."

"If it is, you do lead a boring life." She smiled at him and shook her head in wonder. "I'm amazed there isn't one particular woman in your life right now."

"There is definitely one particular woman in my

life right now." He kissed her again on her throat and shoulders.

Through the night they made love and at dawn she fell asleep in his arms. Sometime later, she stirred and looked down at Garrett. The sheet was across his waist, leaving his chest bare. Even in sleep, his looks fascinated her.

She had no regrets. Garrett excited her more than any man she had ever known. He was intelligent, interesting, fun to be with, exceedingly sexy. She thought she could still keep her heart intact as long as she ended the intimacy when they returned to their regular lives in Texas.

But could she do that? She was realistic enough to know that she was not wildly in love. She was certain she could say no to intimacy.

She leaned down to kiss his shoulder so lightly her lips barely brushed him. His arm circled her waist, pulling her down against him as he slowly opened his eyes. He rolled over while she opened her mouth to tell him good morning. Before she could say a word he kissed her and all conversation was lost.

It was almost two hours later when he held her in his arms while sunshine spilled into the room.

"I have a suggestion for the day," he said. "I'll cook breakfast and then we can ski. Or I'll cook breakfast and then we'll stay right here in the cabin."

She laughed. "I say we cook breakfast and ski because that's what we came here to do. And we've been loving it up for hours."

"And I'm ready to love it up some more," he said, rolling over on top of her to end their discussion.

He finally cooked breakfast at one. They ate beside a

window with a view of the mountains that surrounded the small town.

"Do we have time to ski for an hour?"

"Of course," he replied, looking amused. "It's my plane. We can ski for three hours if you want, or longer."

"One hour will be sufficient and then I'll be ready to go back to Texas."

"One hour it is. But there's no need to rush back to Texas."

"Garrett, it's over."

He paused, gazing into her eyes. He cocked his head to one side. "Don't make up your mind hastily. You might change how you feel."

She shook her head. "No. Last night was special and I wanted it to be with you, but we won't pursue it because that could to lead to heartbreak. I'm not taking that chance."

"You're scared to live, Sophia." His gray eyes darkened slightly. He looked away and a muscle worked in his jaw, a more intense reaction than she would have expected. For an instant, anger flashed like a streak of lightning and then was gone.

"Maybe I'm just exercising caution and waiting for a deep, true love. This weekend was a brief idyll in my steady life."

"You're an artist and I doubt if there is any way you can describe your life as 'steady.'"

"Let's clean up and go ski."

"I have someone who will come in and clean after we're gone. We'll spend our time on the slopes."

She hurried to dress, thinking about their conversation and wondering if she could stick by her declarations. She had never expected to have this night of love and yet she had made the decision clearly and rationally and she had no regrets.

But she began to wonder: Was one of the consequences of her actions last night falling in love with Garrett?

She mulled over the question, unable to answer it. She didn't feel the same toward him as she had before they'd made love for hours. And to her surprise, the night simply made her want to be with him more, not less. Could she stand by her resolutions, do what she knew she should do?

Could she avoid a heartbreak with Garrett? Or was she blindly ignoring the truth that she might be falling in love with him already?

Or, more likely, that she had fallen in love with him that first night she met him?

They skied and returned to his condo by five after eating burgers on the way back. Garrett made a call to his pilot. "He'll be ready. I told him we can be there by six."

"I can be ready in just a few minutes. After all, I didn't bring much."

"I'll call him back and make it thirty minutes from now. Or maybe I won't," he said, his voice dropping. He tossed his phone on a table and crossed to take her into his arms, holding her tightly as he kissed her.

Their passionate kiss lengthened until clothes flew and they made love again with a desperate haste.

By seven, they were airborne. She looked below as twinkling lights disappeared and the night swallowed the plane.

"Garrett, it was a wonderful weekend," she said.

He leaned close to kiss her briefly. When he straightened up, he met her gaze. "It *was* a wonderful weekend," he repeated. "An unforgettable one, Sophia. I hope we have more unforgettable moments together. A lot more," he said.

"I don't think that will happen," she said. "We've both avoided any lasting relationship so I don't expect one to happen now."

"The heart is unpredictable."

"You sound like a romantic," she said, amused.

"That's the first time in my life I've ever been accused of being a romantic."

"Maybe I see a different side to you."

He smiled at her.

"When will you let me paint your portrait?"

"I'd love to have anything you paint, except a painting with myself as the subject. I can't exactly see hanging it in my house."

"Everyone should have a portrait painted. It's for posterity. You'll change your mind, and when you do, remember that I'd like to paint it. You have an interesting face."

"Another first. I've never heard that before either. I think you're seeing different things in me from what everyone else sees."

"I see good things."

"Sophia, listen. I want to be in your life for a long time."

"I'm all for continuing to get to know each other, Garrett," she said carefully.

He leaned close, placing his hands on both arms of her chair. "I hope you never change your mind," he said, startling her with his sincerity, a look of deep sorrow on his face.

"What is it, Garrett?"

He sat back and smiled at her, looking himself again. "I just hope we can keep spending time together."

While they talked, she thought about the past twenty-four hours and was still amazed at how her life had taken an unexpected turn since meeting Garrett.

It was after ten by the time they reached her house. "If you have a moment, come in and I'll show you the studio."

"Sure. Why put off until tomorrow what you can do today?" he teased.

They walked through a wide entry hall that had a twelve-foot-high ceiling. A circular staircase curved to the second floor. Double doors opened to a dining area on one side of the front hall while columns separated the hall from a formal living area.

He paused to look at Louis XVI furniture on the polished oak floor and an elegant marble fireplace. "I'm surprised. I expected you to have something rustic to match your paintings." One of her landscapes hung above the mantel. "That's a superb painting. No wonder you kept it."

"Thank you. I enjoy it. Mountains and a stream—I've been there and I like to look at the painting and remember."

She took his arm. "Come on. I'll show you the kitchen and my studio."

They entered a blue-and-white kitchen with ash woodwork and a casual dining area. "Now I can picture you in your house when I talk to you on the phone," he said.

Switching on lights, she led him into another spacious room. "Here's where I spend most of my time."

He stood looking at her studio with easels, drawing boards, a wide paint-spattered table. Paintings hung on the walls and stood on the floor. Empty frames of various sizes leaned against a wall. Garrett prowled the room and then paused at the large windows overlooking her patio and pool area. Crystal-blue water filled a free-form-shaped pool that had two splashing fountains.

He turned to her. "I like to see where you work. Now do I get to see the bedrooms upstairs?"

She smiled at him. "No, you don't. It's getting late and we've had a long weekend."

"So I'm not allowed to see your bedroom."

"You don't need to," she said, smiling at him as she linked her arm in his.

"I'm having the grand tour tonight but I still want to take you to dinner tomorrow."

"I look forward to it," she said as they walked to her front door.

Before they reached it, he stopped to face her, placing his hands on her waist. "This weekend was incredibly special," he said in a husky voice.

"It was for me," she said, looking up into his gray eyes that mesmerized her as always. Desire filled them and her heart drummed loudly.

"You're special, Sophia. I mean what I say. I never expected to feel the way I do toward you. From the first moment, knowing you hasn't been at all what I expected. So quickly, you've become important to me," he added with a solemn expression.

"So you had expectations about meeting me? That's interesting." In some ways, she wanted to cover her ears and stop hearing his words because she was falling in love with him and it scared her. But Garrett's words wrapped around her heart. He, too, looked as if he were wrestling with something, so their attraction was taking an emotional toll on him, too. "You've become important to me, too, Garrett," she whispered. She stepped close, going on tiptoe to kiss him.

Instantly his arms banded her waist and he leaned over her, kissing her hard.

As if unable to control her own actions, she twisted free his buttons swiftly, her fingers shaking, while she still kissed him.

He tossed off clothes and peeled away hers and in seconds, he lifted her while he kissed her.

"Protection, Garrett?"

"I have it," he said. When he picked her up again, she locked her long legs around him as he lowered her on his thick rod to make love to her.

Crying out, she climaxed, going over an edge while colors exploded behind her closed eyelids.

He shuddered with his release. "Sophia, love," he said in a gruff, husky voice. The endearment made her heart miss a beat.

She moved with him until they both began to catch their breath. He gave her light kisses and finally set her on her feet.

"Now I do need to be directed to a bathroom somewhere in this house."

"There's one in the guest bedroom at the back of the hall, across from my studio. Clean towels will be out."

He leaned down to kiss her again, then gathered his clothes. She picked up hers, pausing to watch him walk away. He was muscled and fit. He looked strong, masculine, sexy. Her gaze ran down his smooth back, over hard buttocks and then down his muscled legs. He was hard, solid and breathtaking.

She gathered her things and headed to her own bathroom off her studio.

In a short time she returned to the front hall to find

him waiting by the door. When she reached him, he pulled her close to kiss her tenderly.

"I don't suppose I'm going to be invited to stay the rest of the night."

"As adorable as you are, no invitation is forthcoming."

"Let me take you to breakfast again. I'll want to see you in the morning."

She laughed. "Garrett, that's crazy. And I can't go. I have appointments."

"I want to be with you."

"Again, Garrett, this has been a special weekend I'll never forget."

He kissed her again. When they moved apart, he opened the door and stepped outside. "Thanks for going with me."

After he left, she locked up and went upstairs to her bedroom.

Had she just done the most foolish thing of her life by making love with him? She hoped not. There was no denying he was becoming more significant to her all the time. In her room she spun around just as she had outside the restaurant in the falling snow in Colorado. Exuberance, excitement, memories dazzled her. Shoving aside worries, she thought about their loving, remembering Garrett in moments of passion, his magnificent body, his tenderness, his heat and sexiness. His kisses held promises and temptation. It had been one of the most wonderful weekends in her life.

She sang as she hurried to shower, moving as if by rote while she replayed the weekend in her mind.

Was this love? Was she already wildly in love with him?

Five

A car was parked at the gate of Garrett's estate. As his lights shone on it, the door opened and Edgar stepped out, patiently waiting.

Garrett's heart dropped. He knew why Edgar was waiting for him.

He put the car in Park and stepped out to walk to Edgar. His mind raced. Had Edgar already told Sophia? Was he here at Sophia's request or because of his own anger over Garrett's duplicity?

The gatekeeper stood in the doorway of the gatehouse. "I tried to reach you on your cell," he said.

"It's all right," Garrett said. "I know Mr. Hollingworth." He turned to shake hands with Edgar, relieved slightly to see Edgar offer his hand.

"Sorry, Garrett," Edgar said. "I know this is a late hour, but I want to talk to you in person. This isn't something to deal with over the phone."

"That's fine. Come up to the house and we'll talk. You can follow me in."

"Thanks."

Garrett returned to his car to drive through the gates. Edgar turned in behind him. At least he had been civil, which was a hopeful sign. More than he expected from Sophia when she discovered the truth about his connections.

At the house, he led Edgar into the library where a decanter of brandy and small crystal glasses sat on a mahogany table.

"Would you care for brandy?"

"Yes, thank you."

Shedding his jacket, Garrett poured two brandies although he had no interest in drinking. He handed a glass to Edgar.

"You're more than CEO of a Houston property management firm," Edgar said. "You're CFO of Delaney Enterprises in Dallas. I assume the property management business here is a sideline of yours."

"It actually was started by my dad," Garrett said. He looked at Edgar, waiting for the rest. When Edgar didn't continue, Garrett asked, "Have you told Sophia yet?"

"No."

"I'll tell you what I'm doing here and why I haven't told her about my connection," Garrett said, proceeding to run through his history with the Delaneys and his purpose in meeting Sophia.

"I intended to get to know her so she would at least let someone talk to her about meeting with Will Delaney. So far, she won't even talk to their lawyer, much less to any of them. Edgar, I don't know what details she's told you, but she stands to lose an enormous inheritance and cost the Delaney brothers theirs. They are as innocent in this as she is."

"I know," Edgar said, swirling his brandy in the snifter and then looking up to meet Garrett's gaze. "She's told me. That's why I'm here. First, I don't want her hurt."

"I don't want to hurt her either. I hate keeping this secret from her. I've come to care very much about Sophia. To be honest, I've thought about resigning, but I have deep obligations to the Delaney family."

"Don't resign. I want you to succeed. I want Sophia to get her inheritance. It's absurd for her to toss aside that kind of money. I came to see you to learn what you intend and to make certain you're not going to hurt her. I feel like a father to her."

"I will try in every way I can to avoid hurting her."

"Sophia is very cautious with men. Therefore, she's rather naive. As far as the Delaneys go—I hope to heaven you succeed in making her listen."

"They want to know her and want her in their family. But they didn't even know she existed until the reading of Argus's will."

"Why am I not surprised. That man was arrogant."

"There's one grandchild, Caroline Delaney, who is five years old. This will hurt her, too," he said, pulling out his phone and touching it. He crossed the room to show a photo to Edgar.

"Great heavens!" Edgar exclaimed, taking the phone to stare at the picture. "Except for the curly hair, she looks like Sophia. Actually, Sophia and this half brother bear a strong resemblance."

"Yes, they do."

"Does Sophia know about the child?"

"She has to because Caroline is in the will. There's a

trust for her. Caroline's mother walked out when Caroline was a baby and the oldest brother, Adam, was her father. When he was killed in a plane crash, Will became Caroline's guardian. Caroline has lost enough in this life." Garrett put away the phone, retrieved his brandy and sat again.

Edgar sipped his brandy. "I'll do what I can, but I can't keep her from looking you up. I'm amazed she hasn't already. She must like you and take you at your word."

"I think she's been reassured because Jason Trent knows me. She knows I have a business here and you had already met me. I've had her to my house and now we've spent a weekend together."

"Believe me, that's unlike her. She's very cautious and I'm sure she's already told you why."

"Argus again and his treatment of her mother. I'm not Argus or even close, and not one drop of his blood runs in my veins."

"True. I hope you can talk some sense into her for her own sake. It's absurd for her to toss aside that fabulous inheritance. She doesn't have the kind of money to be so blasé about it."

"Thanks for letting me try to work this out. I just want her to talk to Will and to think about what she's doing to them and herself."

"If I can help in any manner, let me know." Edgar took another long sip of brandy and set down his glass. "I'll go now. I'm relieved to hear your purpose and I hope you succeed. I'll stay out of this until I'm asked to do otherwise."

He offered his hand and they shook again. "Thanks, Edgar. I appreciate it. I intend to tell her soon and I hope that doesn't end her speaking to me."

"I can't help you much if it does. Sophia has a mind of her own and is quite independent. She grew up that way."

At the front door, Garrett walked out on the porch. "Take care, Edgar. The gates will be open."

"Good luck. I will try to get her to listen to reason. Sooner or later she will tell me when she learns the truth about you."

As Garrett watched him drive away, his cell phone rang. It was Will Delaney.

"How did the weekend go?" he asked.

"It was fine. But suppose you had called in the middle of a moment when I would not have wanted to talk to you?"

"You wouldn't have answered your phone," Will said with a laugh.

"I'm actually glad you called. I've been thinking about it, Will. I don't want to accept any pay for this."

"What the hell? Is there something in the water in Houston that makes people not want money? She won't take her inheritance. Now you don't want your pay."

"Just accept that I am off the payroll on this. I'm doing the Delaneys a favor. It's free, gratis," he said, feeling a faint degree better that he wasn't taking money for keeping his purpose from Sophia. But he still hated being secretive.

"I'm not going to argue with you. You're a big boy now and if you don't want money, okay. We can renegotiate your salary."

"Don't push me, Will," Garrett said. He knew Will was teasing and being flip, but he didn't feel like horsing around.

"Sorry, Garrett, if this has turned sour for you. Okay,

no pay. We're all grateful as hell, as usual. So it went well?"

"Yes, it went well. I'll call you when I have something solid to report. Night, Will."

He clicked off. His thoughts shifted to Edgar and then to Sophia. Tomorrow night he had to tell her the truth. Would the intimacy they had shared this weekend be a strong enough bond to keep her from despising him? He couldn't answer his own question.

Sleep eluded him again. He mulled over the fact that she had been a virgin. He was the first man in her life, which shook him. She had strong feelings about intimacy and had avoided it all these years. He hadn't expected that and now, not telling her his connection to the Delaneys seemed even worse.

Why had she changed her mind this weekend? How deep did feelings run between them? Were they deep enough to withstand the shock she was going to receive?

Could she forgive him? If she did agree to meet the Delaneys and give them a chance, would it mean that she was willing to give her relationship with him a chance? Garrett clenched his fists. He was anxious to tell her while at the same time, he dreaded the moment. The fact that she had let him make love to her made him feel a bond with her that he hadn't experienced before. Thinking about making love last night, his thoughts shifted and memories flooded him until he had to get out of bed and do something physical because he couldn't sleep. The prospect of flying home and resigning still tempted him, yet he couldn't do that either. Obligations to the Delaneys, to Will, to memories of his father's wishes were all too strong. Now the Delaney legacy made him sink even deeper into his obligations to them.

He had to stay and confess his ties to the Delaneys to Sophia.

Not one thing about meeting Sophia had turned out the way he had expected. The most certain thing he knew, though, was that he wanted her with him. He missed her and wanted her in his arms and in his bed right now. He conjured up the memory of her spinning around in the snow, big flakes on her silky black hair and lashes and coat, her smile, her bubbling enthusiasm and zest for life. He ached to hold her again and he would remember the weekend all his life.

Would the truth destroy his budding relationship with Sophia? Or could he make her see how much he wanted to be with her even though he had kept this secret from her?

He had basically lied to her about who he was. How could he make it up to her? Would she even let him try?

Sophia tossed restlessly in bed. She missed Garrett, but she was annoyed with herself for reacting in such a manner. The weekend still dazzled her, memories bubbling up constantly that enveloped her and carried her away. Garrett had changed her feelings about intimacy. Had her feelings for Garrett become so strong, she was changing her basic views of life?

They would be together again in less than twenty-four hours. He would have stayed tonight if she had let him. Those two things made her wonder: Was she rushing headlong into a life like her mother's? Had Garrett so easily demolished all the barriers she kept around her heart?

Realizing that she needed a distraction from thinking about Garrett, she switched on a light and got up to paint, losing herself in her task and driving all thought of him away until morning came.

Monday night she dressed eagerly, trying various outfits and finally selecting a red crepe blouse with a low-cut rounded neckline and straight skirt that had a slit on one side. She pinned the sides of her hair up, letting it fall in the back.

Her pulse raced with anticipation and she was impatient to see him.

When she greeted him, he stepped inside and swept her into his arms. Words were lost as he kissed her. She locked her arms around him and kissed him in return.

Finally she stepped back. "Another minute and I won't look presentable to go out to dinner."

"That's impossible." He held her waist and stepped back to look at her. "You're beautiful, just perfect."

"I think you're the perfect one," she said, thinking his charcoal suit made his gray eyes appear darker. "I'm ready."

"So am I," he said in a husky voice, referring to more than just dinner.

"We're going to dinner. You promised," she reminded him.

"Yes, I did. We'll go eat and then we're coming back here and I'm going to kiss you the way I want to."

His words made her tingle and she smiled at him.

He took her arm to escort her to a sleek black sports car. She was surprised it wasn't his chauffeur and his limousine, wondering why he preferred driving. Was it because he expected to stay at her house a long time tonight when he took her home?

She wasn't exactly sure how she felt about that, despite the desire for him that had been burning through her since they'd last made love.

They drove through posts and a wrought-iron fence, winding up a drive past splashing fountains and tall pines with lights high in the branches. As they stopped in front of a canopied walk and he gave the keys to a valet, he took her arm. Lights twinkled in all the bushes and over the restaurant, creating a festive atmosphere.

Inside, a large bouquet of four dozen red and yellow roses in a sparkling crystal vase on a marble table stood in the center of the entryway. A maître d' met them, talked briefly to Garrett and led them to a table in a secluded corner that overlooked the dance floor on one side and a terrace on the other. Beyond the terrace were sloping grounds to a well-lit pond with more lights in the trees. Soft piano music played and a few couples were already on the small dance floor.

"I've never eaten here before, Garrett. I've heard of this place, but just haven't been here. It's lovely."

"The food is great. I think you'll like it." A candle flickered in the center of the linen-covered table. Garrett reached across to take her hand. Candlelight was reflected in his gray eyes and her gaze dropped to his mouth. "The weekend was special," he said in a husky voice.

"It was for me, you know that," she replied breathlessly, studying him as he watched her. He had one of the most interesting faces and she wished he would let her paint his portrait. The only problem was that she would want to keep it, and that was the last thing she needed in her house right now, especially if she was trying to slow things down.

"I brought you something to remind you of the weekend and to let you know that it was special for me," he said, handing her a small package.

Surprised, she looked up and smiled. "How sweet you are. You know you didn't need to do this."

She untied a silver ribbon and then unwrapped blue paper on a small box. When she opened it, another velvet box was inside. She removed it and took out a thin gold filigree bracelet.

"Garrett, it's beautiful," she said, touched and surprised. She looked up at him and then took it out to slip it on, turning her wrist as the candlelight highlighted the gold. "Thank you. It's lovely and I'll treasure it."

"Enjoy it, Sophia, and remember the fun we had."

"Of course I will," she said, picking up his hand and leaning forward to brush a light kiss across his knuckles. He inhaled, his chest expanding while desire burned in the depths of his eyes.

All through dinner and later as they danced, desire kept her tingly. Dancing with him was as much fun as everything else. She enjoyed the fast dances; the slow dancing was sexy, tantalizing, making her want to love again. When they stopped and she looked up to meet his gaze, he appeared to be thinking about the same thing she'd been thinking about.

Garrett had a thick steak while she had lobster tail with white wine. Her appetite fled as she watched him in the flickering candlelight. Garrett had ensnared her heart. There was no way she could keep things light with him or hold to her resolution to avoid a relationship. He was important to her and he turned her insides out just looking at him.

By ten, when Garrett asked her if she was ready to leave, she nodded.

At her house, she invited Garrett inside.

"You've had the tour, so would you like a drink—a cup of hot chocolate, soda?"

"If you have iced tea, I'll take that."

"Two iced teas it is," she said, heading for the kitchen. She crossed the room to get out glasses.

"Have a seat and I'll get our drinks. We can go where it's more comfortable."

Garrett moved closer and turned her to face him. "Sophia," he said in a husky voice, and her heart skipped. He leaned down to kiss her while his arm held her waist tightly.

The moment he touched her, her insides clenched and her pulse jumped. She hugged him tightly in return while her intentions to say no to making love vanished.

Nothing seemed as important as kissing and loving him.

"Now you'll have to show me a bedroom," he said, kissing her throat.

"There's one down the hall on this floor," she said, taking his hand to lead him to the bedroom where he stood her on her feet as he continued kissing her. His hands moved deftly over zippers and buttons, and her skirt floated to her ankles where she stepped out of it.

"This time we're taking it nice and slow," he said, taking time to shower kisses on her. He loved her with deliberation, trying to pleasure her and heighten desire every way he could until she was writhing beneath his touch, aching for him.

"Garrett, come here," she whispered, reaching for him.

He slipped on a condom and lowered himself, slowly filling her, withdrawing and entering again while she arched beneath him.

His loving was slow, a sweet torment that fanned the fires he had already ignited.

He was beaded with sweat, trying to maintain control until finally he let go and loved furiously.

She cried out as she climaxed and in seconds he shuddered with his release.

Gradually her heartbeat returned to normal and her breathing grew quiet. They helped each other up and went to shower together, drying each other off only to return to bed. He pulled her into his embrace, holding her while he combed her hair with his fingers.

"Garrett, I didn't know it could be this way," she confessed. "I couldn't say no to you."

"I hope you never can," he whispered, kissing her temple while he held her against his heart with his arms wrapped around her. "This is perfect, Sophia."

"You might as well stay tonight. There's no reason not to."

"I'm glad to hear you say that. I'm surprised you asked me."

"I surprised myself, but it seems logical. And my bracelet is beautiful. Thank you again."

"Just remember our weekend together."

"I will always. There's no way I can forget it."

He gazed into her eyes. "I hope you don't. It was special to me." He kissed her lightly. Though he'd told her many times before, his words thrilled her. She ran her hands over his shoulders, relishing being with him.

At two in the morning, he partially sat up. "I'm ready now for that cup of hot chocolate you offered. Is it still in the offering?"

"Of course. You have to wait a minute because I'm putting on a robe."

"That takes away the fun."

"Otherwise, we'll never get to the hot chocolate."

"True enough."

She stood, wrapping herself in a comforter and going to get a robe. "I'll meet you in the kitchen."

He grinned and waved, his gaze roaming over her as if mentally peeling away the comforter.

"You look gorgeous."

"It's my beautiful gold bracelet," she replied, holding out her arm and letting the bracelet catch glints of light. Smiling, she left to go upstairs and get her best robe, a black velvet robe with a silk lining. She brushed her hair and went down.

When she entered the kitchen, Garrett already had mugs with steaming cocoa on the table. Dressed in his white shirt and slacks again, he gazed at her, then walked to meet her and place his hands on her waist. His white shirt was unbuttoned halfway and she wanted to run her fingers through the hair on his chest. He had turned the fancy French cuffs back and he looked sexy.

"You look far too gorgeous for that to be called a bathrobe. And far too sexy for that to not be for the benefit of some man."

"You know absolutely there hasn't been a man—until now. It's my best warm and comfy bathrobe."

"I'm glad you said 'until now' and I hope it stays that way."

"Garrett, I've warned you about that from the beginning."

He leaned down to kiss her long and hard. Her heart raced as if it were the first time. She couldn't get enough of him. Fighting an inner battle between what she wanted and what she thought she should do, she shifted away.

"We're going to drink hot chocolate, remember?" she said breathlessly, placing her hand against his chest.

He still held her. "Sophia, you're important to me.

I know we haven't known each other long, but that really doesn't matter. You're essential and I want you in my life."

While her heart drummed, his words held her enthralled. "Saturday night wouldn't have happened if you hadn't been very important to me."

"I'm glad. Don't forget what I've said."

"Garrett, you've said that to me before. What am I missing?"

"Before we sit to drink our hot chocolate, I want to talk to you and I hope you'll listen to everything I have to say."

She looked at him and realized that whatever it was he was about to tell her, it wasn't good. "What is it, Garrett? Go ahead and tell me what's troubling you," she said, puzzled, wondering what he wanted to talk about.

"We've become friends, haven't we?"

"Yes, of course. But more than friends, Garrett. Lovers."

"Good. I want to keep it that way."

"What are you getting at?" she asked, growing chilled. What had he been keeping from her that might change her feelings for him? "What do you want to talk about?"

"I want you to promise me you'll listen and keep an open mind."

"I'll listen and I'll try to keep an open mind unless you're going to tell me you're married with a family," she said stiffly. Suddenly, all her fears about rushing into intimacy with him came back to her. All her life she had been cautious, but she threw caution to the wind when Garrett came into her life. And she had a feeling she was about to find out that she'd made a terrible mistake.

He shook his head. "Nothing like that."

Relief was slight because whatever he intended to tell her, it was serious. "I'll try to keep an open mind," she said, though she could already feel the walls closing down around her heart. "But I can't make any promises."

Six

Garrett framed her face with his hands and she watched as he took a deep breath. "I was asked to meet you and get to know you. I was hired to do so, actually, but I've told them I won't take the money. I swear I never expected it to turn out this way at all. I didn't dream I would get any closer to you than I had to in order to talk to you."

"You were hired? To meet me? I don't understand," she said, confusion flooding her. Garrett was struggling with his words, and he wasn't giving her information fast enough. "Answer me, Garrett! Who hired—" She stopped speaking and stared at him, her confusion changing to burning fury. There was only one group of people in the world who would have to hire someone to try to get her to meet with them. "No! It's the Delaneys, isn't it?"

"Yes, it's the Delaneys. Please, Sophia, you have to believe me. I never thought I, we would—"

"Damn you, Garrett," she said, astounded at his pretense and the advantage he had taken of her. She was furious with herself for letting down her guard. "I promised to listen and keep an open mind, but I'm not going to now. Everything you've done has been a sham. You've been conniving and false from the start," she accused. "All that asking about my family, listening while I told you about my father—you're as bad as he was," she said, shaking with rage. "You knew! You knew all the time who Argus was and what he had done! You knew how I grew up. You knew everything when you met me and passed yourself off as a Houston businessman."

"I am a Houston businessman. I own that business."

"How are you connected with the Delaneys?" she blurted, startled to hear he actually had the Houston business.

"I'm the CFO of Delaney Enterprises."

She felt as if he had delivered a blow to her. "So the best friend you talked about, the family obligations—that's all the Delaneys, isn't it?" She clenched her fists. "I'm not going to listen to you. Everything you've done has been underhanded and low. How could you?" she cried.

"Sophia, by denying your heritage and your inheritance, you're hurting innocent people and you're hurting yourself."

"You can't possibly justify your actions." She thought of what had happened between them in Colorado, devastation washing over her like a crushing wave. "How you must have laughed after this weekend. You seduced me for the Delaneys," she said, grinding out the words, tears of anger and hurt threatening, adding to her fury.

"No, I did not. I meant what I've said to you, Sophia. I swear. I meant what I said about how special this weekend was for me—about how special you are to me."

"Oh, please," she snapped, hating him for what he'd done and angry with herself for tossing aside all caution where Garrett had been concerned. She was shaking and hurting all over, and she wanted nothing more than to get rid of him and make sure she never had to lay eyes on him again. "You can get out, Garrett. Out of my house and out of my life."

"I'm not going until you listen to me and hear my side of the story."

"Get out of here," she cried. "I don't want to see you or talk to you. I want you out of my life." She tried to slip the bracelet off her wrist, her hands shaking as she fumbled. She finally succeeded, throwing it at him. He caught it and slowly put it into his pocket, never taking his eyes off her.

"I just want you to listen for a moment," he said, speaking quietly. "You're harming yourself as much as you're hurting them and they haven't done any more than you have. All they did was end up with Argus Delaney as their father. You can't select your parents, and neither could they. So why are you doing this to them, Sophia?"

"I already told you. I don't want anything from Argus Delaney. He never gave me love or attention or even acknowledgment that I was his daughter. Never," she declared bitterly, tears over Garrett's betrayal blinding her eyes as they spilled faster than she could wipe them away. "My father gave us money as a man gives cash to a prostitute. I'm not turning down the money to hurt my half brothers. I'm refusing it because it's the only way I can reject Argus Delaney. He gave it out of guilt at the end of his life, and I will do nothing to exonerate the way he treated me or my mother."

Garrett reached out to touch her and she jerked away from him as if he had scalded her with his touch.

"This isn't about them," she said. "It's about him. All those years from the time I was born until I was in my twenties, he treated me as if I was nothing. I'm not trying to hurt them."

"But you are hurting them. Can't you see? And not just your half brothers. Sophia, there's a grandchild. An adorable little girl, Caroline, who someday will inherit Delaney money. You're hurting that child."

Momentarily startled, she stared at Garrett. "There's a grandchild mentioned in the will. A trust was left for her, which has nothing to do with these inheritances. So how could this affect her?"

"Eventually, she'll inherit money left by her uncles. It's not as big a thing with Caroline, but she's in the family and will inherit family money," he said, pulling out his phone and holding it out for Sophia to see. "Here's Caroline with Will, who is her guardian since her father was killed. Look at it, Sophia. Here are two of the people you're hurting."

She snapped her mouth closed and looked at a picture of a beautiful child with long, black, curly hair and huge brown eyes. Shocked, Sophia stared. The little girl looked like her at a young age. She could see the family resemblance between herself and both the child and the smiling, handsome man in the picture.

"I hadn't thought about the future for her." She continued to stare at the picture, suddenly struck by the fact that she had a family, a family that she had never met, a family that looked very much like her. There was no doubt they were all related. Shaken, she couldn't stop staring at the picture—until she looked at the man who was holding it. Her hurt deepened and she walked away from Garrett to put space between them.

"They have money. The Delaneys are worth billions. This isn't going to hurt any of them." She spun around to glare at him, her anger returning. "If they don't get this inheritance, they'll still be enormously wealthy. They are young and into enough enterprises. They will make more money than they even know what to do with. I want no part of my father or anything that belonged to him. Not a dollar—not a fortune. I will have no part of him."

"He'll never know," Garrett answered, putting away his phone. "Your father is dead now, Sophia. You're not hurting him. The people whose lives you are affecting are Will, Zach, Ryan and Caroline," Garrett said quietly. "Sophia, they didn't even know about your existence— Don't punish them when they haven't snubbed you. When they found out they had a sister, they wanted to meet you. They feel you're part of the family and all of you should be united. Aside from the money, they would have tried to meet you and bring you into the family. They are great guys in spite of their father. They don't want to hurt you. They want you to have your money as much as they would like to have theirs. And they want to meet their sister."

"So they sent you to trick me into meeting them."

"There was no tricking you. They tried to meet you openly. Will called. Zach flew here. You've rejected every contact, including their attorney."

Sophia was losing her patience with Garrett, and

she couldn't stand here and have this conversation with him any longer. "I don't see why you are still standing here when you know you're unwanted," she said coldly, her eyes still blurry from tears that streamed down her cheeks. "Once again, I don't care about the Delaney brothers' inheritances or about meeting them. I don't want to see you again, and I never want to see the Delaneys. I want you to go. You deceived me, Garrett."

"You're not going to listen or give me any kind of chance, are you?"

"How could you do this?" she lashed out, her voice a hiss. She wanted him to get out of her house and her life. Why couldn't he understand?

"I did it because those guys are important to me. And all they want is for you to give them a chance. But I don't want to lose you," he said. Her burning anger had turned to a chill. She shook and couldn't stop tears from falling.

"Get out, Garrett. Just go. You can't change my mind, and you and I are through."

"Sophia, don't do this. You're being stubborn and foolish. If you don't want the money for yourself, give it to charity and do some good with it. You don't have to keep it or live on it."

"There is nothing you can say that will make me change my mind. I don't ever want to meet my half brothers. The only thing we have in common is Argus Delaney and nothing else. Garrett, get it through your head—I don't want to have anything to do with any part of my father, and those half brothers are all part of him."

"You're part of him, Sophia."

"Don't remind me. If I could do anything to erase that, I would." She walked toward the door, opening it to make it very clear that she needed him to leave. "You have to go now."

"Why the hell are you being so selfish about this?" he said. Momentarily, she was taken aback by his harsh accusation and then her anger surged again.

"Selfish? Haven't you been listening when I've talked about my father? His world revolved around him. He thought only of himself. His ego was enormous. Don't accuse me of being selfish. He took the prize."

"But what would it hurt to meet them? There's no way you can be harmed by a meeting. You're being stubborn and unreasonable about this—spiteful and hurtful for no reason. Argus will never know, Sophia. You are not getting back at your father," Garrett said, his voice rising.

"How dare you. How dare you call me spiteful and hurtful after what you've just done to me. In case I haven't made it abundantly clear, Garrett, I don't want to see you again ever."

"Sophia, I don't want to lose you. You're important to me and I thought I was to you. I thought we had something special between us. Other than my connections with the Delaneys, I've been open and truthful with you."

"Other than your connections with the Delaneys? How can you discount that? That is actually the first thing you should have told me about yourself. Because the problem now, Garrett, is that I don't believe you or trust you, and I never will. Get out of my life."

"I'm sorry, Sophia. I'm sorry about everything. About the way this worked out, about how long I kept the truth from you. Just please promise me that you'll think about this and stop having such a closed mind."

Sophia wasn't even going to grace his request with a

response. Instead, she walked out of the room. He followed and caught up with her at the door.

"Just think about what I've said to you. Give some thought to your half brothers who have done nothing to you." When she refused to look at him, he paused for a moment. "Maybe, Sophia, you're more like Argus than you care to admit."

"How dare you, Garrett!" she cried. His words cut like a knife. How could she possibly have given this man her body? Her heart? What on earth was she thinking? "Get out of my life!"

"That isn't what I want to do. I don't want things to end this way between us."

"There is no 'us,' Garrett."

"There was, and there can be, if you'll just give me a chance to explain. I put off telling you about the Delaneys because I was scared of losing you. What I feel for you is real."

"I can't believe you care."

He clenched his fists. "What I want is you in my arms, and in my life. What I feel for you, I've never felt for any woman. I can't tell you how many times I thought about calling Will and resigning. But I didn't, because I believed I was doing the right thing—both for you, and for them."

"Goodbye, Garrett," she said, unwilling to listen to another second of his plea.

"I wish you viewed this differently. You're stirring up a storm when you could have so much joy and give so much joy. And you're doing it for the wrong reasons. Actually, reason doesn't even enter into it. You're blindly striking out and trying to hurt whoever you can. Listen, if I had thought I could be up front with you from the first moment, I would have been. But I can see now that I was right. You wouldn't have talked to me, and so I did the only thing I could to get near you. You have a closed mind. You want me out of your life? I'm out," he stated coldly. He turned and left in long strides.

Sophia slammed her heavy door and sagged against it, sobbing and shaking. She hurt badly in every way.

Garrett had betrayed her—she couldn't perceive anything else. Their lovemaking had simply been a means to an end, nothing more. When they had made love, he hadn't been emotionally involved—he had been working. But as swiftly as that thought came, she replayed the pain in his voice as he confessed to her, and she believed his emotions were real.

Yet how could she trust him now?

She heard his car and then it was gone. And with that, Garrett vanished out of her life.

She sat on the nearest chair and cried. Hurt was overwhelming. Heartbroken, she hated herself for being duped just as much as she hated Garrett for deceiving her. How blind she had been to Garrett's purpose.

His accusations echoed in her thoughts—*you're selfish; you're blindly striking out and trying to hurt whoever you can.*

Was he right? Was she being selfish?

He had not succeeded or even come close to getting her to consider meeting the Delaneys. So would Garrett continue trying, or was he giving up?

Would she ever see him again? And could she admit to herself that after everything he had done to her, after everything that had happened, the possibility of never seeing him was the worst part of all of this?

Garrett slid behind the wheel and took deep breaths. Desperate at the thought of losing Sophia, he had been tempted to just grasp her shoulders and force her to talk to him. But where the Delaneys were concerned, Sophia had shut off reason.

Her actions shocked him even though he had known about her feeling rejected beforehand, and had heard her bitterness when she talked about the Delaneys, particularly her father.

Anger churned his insides. Along with fury was an uncustomary hurt. He had enjoyed being with her more than any other woman he had known. He wasn't ready for the hurt of losing her. He wasn't ready for the fallout from telling the truth, yet he had been compelled to do so. How could she be so stubborn?

Clenching his teeth until his jaw hurt, he drove home, charging into the empty house and tossing down his keys. Yanking off his jacket as he headed to his room, he tried to compose his thoughts and get a grip on his stormy emotions.

He'd always thought Will was the most stubborn Delaney—until now. Sophia was more stubborn than Will because Will would at least listen to reason and if you got through to him, he would cooperate. Sophia, on the other hand, turned deaf ears to his arguments.

He thought about the night and her passion. It was as if he had been with a different woman when they had made love. A warm, loving, passionate woman. He hurt and hurt for her.

He swore quietly, pacing his room, glaring at the phone. He needed to break the news to Will, but he wasn't ready yet.

Would she ever give him another chance to talk to her about the Delaneys—or to make it up to her? He doubted it and he didn't care to hang around with unreasonable expectations.

He went to the kitchen to get a cold beer. Reeling with anger and frustration, Garrett popped the top and took a drink, feeling the cold liquid wash down his throat.

Procrastinating, Garrett stared at the window. He did not want to call Will or any other Delaney. Yet he had to. What would he do if he were in Will's place? What could he suggest Will and his brothers do now? In future years, after the inheritances were dispersed to other places and no longer an issue, then would she meet with the Delaneys? The brothers truly wanted to know their sister, and Garrett knew they wouldn't stop trying. Surely then she would think more rationally about them and give them a chance.

But would she ever give *him* another chance?

Garrett paced the floor and sipped his beer while he thought. All the time he had argued with her, he had wanted to just wrap his arms around her and ask her to forgive him, believe him and go back to the way things had been. He knew that was unrealistic, but he wanted her badly and he hurt now in a manner he had never hurt before in his life.

Reluctantly, he picked up the phone. Will answered on the second ring.

"Will, it's Garrett."

"You're running true to schedule, waking me in the wee hours of the morning. What's the deal?"

"Here's the latest," he said, pausing. This was the second-hardest thing he had ever had to tell someone. "I did what I could for you with Sophia."

"Whoa, Garrett. You told her who you are?"

"Yes, I did. I had to. I think waiting longer would have made it worse and it's bad enough anyway."

"Go ahead," Will said, his voice becoming gruff, the

disappointment showing. "I'm not sure I want to hear, but I know I have to. This doesn't sound good."

"It's not," Garrett declared. "She's adamant about her decision. She still won't meet with any of you," he said, pain rippling through him as he remembered her cold remarks to him.

"Dammit, I thought you were getting close to her— I thought this would work."

"I did get damn close to her, but the instant she learned the truth... You can't imagine her fury. She doesn't want anything to do with me or any Delaney. Will, I did my damnedest with her."

"I'm sure you did. I'm disappointed, but not with you. You always give a job your best."

"We were getting along great and I thought I could safely tell her. I was wrong, but I don't think she would have been any different if I had waited a year. She won't listen to reason. She's stubborn, determined and filled with hate for Argus. Because of that, Sophia will pass up the inheritance and hurt herself along with all of you. I've been shocked by the depth of her anger toward your dad. It's monumental."

"Garrett, I gotta ask," he said. "I've been thinking about you giving up your pay for this. Do you care about her?"

Silence stretched between them. Garrett didn't want to answer Will, but he knew his silence was telling.

"Dammit," Will said. "We didn't want you getting hurt in the cross fire."

"Forget it, Will. None of us—not any of you, Sophia or even I—expected us to get involved. That's beside the point here."

"Sorry. That's bad news. When the time is up on the

inheritances, and we still want to meet her, do you think she'll at least meet us and let us try to be a family?"

"I can't answer that."

"We all want to know her. You liked her, so in the right circumstances, I suppose we would, too."

"Yes, you would. She's like you in some ways, like Zach in others. She's stubborn as hell—definitely a Delaney."

Another heavy silence ensued. "What do you suggest as a next step?" Will finally asked.

"I've been thinking about it and the only thing I can come up with is to go back to your lawyer. Or get a different lawyer and see if he can reason with her."

"Like I said, she won't even talk to our attorney. She has her attorney talk to our attorney."

"All right, but get him to tell her attorney everything you want her to know. Try to get him to convince her attorney this is in her best interests, which it is. Also, try to get across that you want to know her and include her in the family."

"We'll do that."

"How can her attorney not want to argue in your favor when the size of the inheritance is so huge?" Garrett asked.

"I don't know. Maybe a female attorney might get farther."

"I don't think it'll matter. Man or woman, just get someone who is very clever and competent."

"We'll try. Don't come home yet. Stay a few days longer and see if Sophia relents and has a change of heart."

"Will, I'm coming home. Sophia doesn't want to talk to me or see me again."

"How could she be this bitter when he provided for them and her mother was in love with him?"

"She hated seeing her mother hurt by him, especially when he wouldn't marry her. As a child she felt shut out and ignored by him."

"That wasn't so different from how he dealt with us. We had nannies, boarding schools. It wasn't until we were adults that he began to show real interest in us."

"She doesn't know that and won't care. Since she's never met any of you, you're not real to her and she is lashing out at him. She's financially independent and she's content with what she has."

"The one person on earth who doesn't want more money and she has to turn out to be our sister."

"Sorry, Will. I failed all of you, but I tried," Garrett said. "Will, other than this facet to her personality, she's great. She truly is. You would like her."

"Too bad she's not one of those people who wants to be reunited with her long-lost relatives."

"Work with your lawyer. Beyond that, I can't think of any way to reach her."

"Thanks, Garrett. I know you tried. I still say you might hang around in case she has a change of heart. Miracles happen and you had a chance to say some good things about us."

"Will, I couldn't say anything about you, much less sing your praises."

"You surely did a little tonight."

"I didn't have much of an opportunity. I'll wait a few days but it's hopeless as far as I can tell."

"Okay, I'll let the others know," he said, and paused. "Damn, thanks seems inadequate if the two of you had something going and then this killed the relationship."

"Don't worry about me."

"Hang in there, Garrett. And keep in touch."

"Sure. Sorry, Will. I'm damned sorry," Garrett repeated.

He told Will goodbye, then raking his fingers through his hair, he swore. As bitter as Sophia had been and as stubborn, he couldn't imagine her changing.

He looked at his phone and pulled up the picture he had taken of her. His anger transformed to pain as he stood mesmerized by the picture of the moment that remained magical in his memory. She looked breathtaking, happy, sexy. He remembered reaching out to pull her into his arms and kiss her, and he longed to feel her against him now. Even though he was angry with her stubborn refusal to open her mind a little, he was torn with guilt about making love to her when he had been deceiving her. There were reasons he deserved her anger. He wanted to hold her right now.

He hurt for the loss. While he hadn't known her long, it had seemed as if she had become a permanent part of his life.

He shook his head and swore again. The familiarity and closeness had been pure delusion. For her to become so furious with him, he must have meant nothing to her.

He couldn't stop glancing at the picture even though he knew the futility of longing to see her. Wasn't going to happen. He ran his thumb over her smiling image. Tonight would she think over what he had said? Or was she almost as angry with him as she was with Argus? Garrett missed her far more than he would have dreamed possible.

There was no going back, no setting aside the Delaneys and having something with Sophia. He might as well start trying to move on with his life.

* * *

Sophia painted until six, knowing she was merely going through the motions until she had to get dressed for some appointments. Her anger was overshadowed by pain over the break with Garrett and the deceit he had practiced. She couldn't believe it— Argus Delaney was still causing her pain even after his death. Garrett's arguments nagged at her, but she didn't want to think about them or consider them in the least. He had completely betrayed her trust—in more ways than one.

She didn't believe for a second that the Delaneys wanted to meet her and would still want to after the deadline had passed. They had to be just like their father and after more money. She was certain greed ruled their lives.

When she went to her closet, she barely glanced at her red suit that she had worn with Garrett. Pulling out a black suit that matched her mood, she stepped out of her robe and began to dress. She tried to put last night out of her mind as she got ready to go to the gallery.

She called Edgar and they agreed to meet for lunch. Friday was the anniversary of the opening of his first gallery and he was celebrating with an open house. He had planned to send invitations to clients with a listing of the artists who would be present, including her. Now she wished she could cancel so she could go to Santa Fe and try to forget Garrett, the Delaneys and everything that had happened since Garrett had come into her life. She wouldn't do that to Edgar, but it was a tempting thought.

At her gallery, she tried to get things done as quickly as possible so she'd be ready to leave Houston as soon as she could. Also, she found that the gallery held memories of being with Garrett.

She had to rush to meet Edgar on time. Standing beside their table, he smiled as she approached.

"Oh, my," he said as soon as she was close. He held her chair for her. "Something is wrong. I take it this is not just a fun lunch."

"You're too astute, Edgar," she said lightly. She sat and picked up a menu although she ate there often with Edgar and knew what she liked. She just needed a moment behind her menu before she told Edgar the whole story. It wasn't going to be easy. Their waiter came and they both ordered. As soon as they were alone, she met Edgar's curious gaze.

"I'll give you a clue. When you're upset, you always fasten your hair up in a tight knot," he said.

Startled, she glanced at him. "I don't," she replied and he shrugged. She could tell he didn't want to argue, but he was probably right. "I didn't even realize."

"We don't notice ourselves sometimes. So tell me—what's the problem?"

"I would really like to go back to Santa Fe. Will it be too big an inconvenience for me to cancel my appearance at your anniversary party? Have you already sent invitations with the names of the artists who will be present?"

"Actually, I have. But if you need to miss, you may be excused."

"I can wait until after the party and then go."

"Is there an emergency?" Edgar asked, looking at her closely.

"No, not at all. I just wanted to get away."

"Taking Garrett Cantrell with you?" Edgar asked and she sucked in her breath.

"No, I'm not," she snapped and then wished she had

not answered so abruptly. "It's over with him, Edgar. He's from Dallas and he was sent by the Delaneys."

"So how did you learn this bit of information?"

"He told me. He was sent to get me to talk to them. I told him how I felt about the Delaneys, particularly my father. I don't want the inheritance. I don't want to meet my half brothers. Garrett tricked me and I never want to see him again," she said.

"Seems as if he didn't trick you if he told you that they sent him."

Just as she opened her mouth to answer, their waiter appeared with lunches. She had no appetite for her tossed salad. She sipped water as she watched the waiter place chicken salad in front of Edgar.

"Edgar," she said as soon as they were alone, her curiosity growing. "You don't sound offended and you don't sound surprised."

Edgar sighed. "Garrett told me, Sophia. I knew why he was here."

"Why on earth didn't you warn me?" she asked, aghast at another betrayal from a man she had trusted all her life.

"You know why, Sophia," Edgar stated, putting down his fork and gazing at her intently. "You and I have been over this and I dropped it because it is your decision, but since it has come up again, I'll make another plea. I hate to see you hurt yourself. And you will be hurting yourself in a huge, lifelong manner that I think you will come to regret. You may be hurting yourself terribly in losing Garrett. He seemed like a good man, Sophia."

"Edgar, I'm shocked. You're my friend. Why did you side with the Delaneys on this? When did you turn against me?"

"Far from 'turning against you,' I want what's in

your best interests and I was thankful when Garrett told me why he was here. Sophia, stop being a wounded child about this."

Edgar's words stung. He had always been a mentor, her champion, always supportive and helpful until this argument about the Delaneys and even then, until now, he had backed off and kept quiet.

"Edgar, you know how Argus Delaney hurt Mom and me."

"That has nothing to do with your brothers."

"They're grown men and probably just like their father. They're half brothers, and they're strangers to me."

"You know there is a grandchild. A little girl who looks very much like you."

"Edgar, these people are worth billions. They're all going to be just fine."

"You don't really enjoy money the way some people do. But you do know how to help others with it. You could put it to so much good use. And what did you do—send Garrett packing?"

"Yes, I did. And he deserved it."

"Sophia, I got the impression that he cares for you deeply. Don't throw everything away because of his mistake. Someday, you might look back with enormous regrets that you may not be able to live with. You can take this inheritance and help so many others who have never been as fortunate as you."

"Edgar, I'm shocked that you and Garrett talked and you didn't tell me. I'm finished here. I don't want to argue this with you. I've had enough arguing with Garrett." She stood, tossed her napkin into her chair, grabbed up her purse and left. She couldn't believe Edgar had known why Garrett was here. Another betrayal that cut deeply.

Tears stung her eyes, adding to her anger. She rushed outside the restaurant.

"Sophia—"

She turned as Edgar appeared. Startled he had caught up with her, she stopped. "Leave me alone, Edgar," she snapped, wiping her eyes.

His blue eyes narrowed. "I daresay those tears are not over me. We've known each other too long. You're crying over Garrett."

"I am not," she blurted, knowing as she said the words that Edgar was right.

Edgar bent down slightly to look into her eyes. "I think you're in love with him."

"Edgar, you're not making me feel any better."

"That's what I'm trying to tell you. You're making a mistake and you'll be miserable. Sophia, don't mess up your life this way. Life can be harsh, cold and lonely. You're tossing away opportunities and family with both hands. And maybe tossing away love."

"I have to go and I don't want to hear this."

"You may not want to hear it, but you know I'm right," he said gently. "I told Garrett that I hoped he succeeded not just because you need to accept your legacy, but because it's time you let someone love you."

"Goodbye," she said, turning away.

"Sophia." Edgar's commanding tone was so unusual she stopped instantly and turned to face him.

"I'll be here if you want me. I suspect Garrett would be, too, if you let him."

She rushed to her car, climbing in and locking the door while tears poured down her cheeks. She couldn't stop her crying. It took several minutes, but finally when her emotions were more under control, she started the car and drove carefully.

When she got home, she changed and went to her studio, losing herself in paints, brushstrokes, colors. As she worked, she thought of the things both Garrett and Edgar had said to her about the Delaneys. *You're harming yourself as much as you're hurting them.... You can't select your parents and you didn't pick Argus.... Why are you doing this to the brothers?*

Garrett's gray eyes had been dark as he'd spoken. His words had cut, yet she couldn't deny that there was truth in them. Was she making mistakes she would regret the rest of her life? Should she take the inheritance and then distribute it to worthwhile causes?

Should she let these brothers—these Delaney men—into her life?

She stopped painting to clean her brushes and then continued cleaning tables and doing housekeeping tasks she had put off. It was all she was suited for at the moment. Her concentration on her painting was poor with her thoughts continually returning to her conversation with Garrett. His words rang in her ears. *I don't want to lose you....*

But he had lost her. She didn't think there was any way she could forgive him for not telling her his purpose from the start. He had been as intimate as a man could be without revealing the truth about himself. That was what hurt most of all. It was the first time she had trusted totally, let go of her caution and doubts, and then found that the whole time she hadn't known the truth about him or why he had wanted to meet her.

Take the money and give it to charity. Do some good with it. You don't have to keep it or live on it.

Edgar had said the same in his own way. But she couldn't see that she was hurting herself— She had no real need of the money.

You're being stubborn and unreasonable about this—spiteful and hurtful for no reason.

Stubborn and unreasonable, spiteful and hurtful. Both Garrett and Edgar had accused her of being selfish.

She washed her hands and put away her brushes, going to her room to look at the letter from the Delaneys' attorney.

You are not getting back at your father.

Was she wrong and both men were right? Would she have huge regrets?

She rubbed her forehead, feeling the beginnings of a headache coming on. Everything had seemed so clear to her when it had first come up, but now she was beginning to wonder.

"Garrett," she whispered, angry with him and missing him all at the same time. Garrett had caused her to rethink her feelings about relationships. Was she about to rethink the whole Delaney situation because of him? She rubbed her hands together in anguish.

Had Garrett gone back to Dallas now, to his life there?

Had there been a woman in his life already? Had his declaration that there wasn't a woman been the truth—or another deceitful statement?

She spent a miserable, restless evening with little sleep that night. The next day, she got out the information from the Delaneys and their attorneys, and the copy of her father's will, which told of the bequest and the conditions.

She sat at her desk and read, studying the legal documents in her quiet house, weighing possibilities that she thought she never would have considered.

Edgar always had her best interests at heart. He had

backed Garrett, hoping Garrett could persuade her to take her legacy.

What she longed to do was see Garrett and talk to him. Facing the truth, she was shocked by her wish. When had Garrett become so important in her life? Could she forgive him? At the moment, she felt no inclination to do so. And even if she did, was he still angry with her? Garrett might not be forgiving. Her spirits sank lower. The pain of her argument with him was not only monumental, it kept growing.

She had never felt so lost in her entire life.

Friday night, for Edgar's anniversary celebration at his gallery, Sophia dressed in a plain, long-sleeved black dress. The neckline dipped to her waist in the back and the skirt ended above her knees. Her hair was looped and piled on her head, held in place with combs. She remembered what Edgar had said about when she wore her hair knotted on her head, but she didn't care. Tonight she felt better with her hair secured and fastened high.

Feeling numb, barely aware of what she was saying or the people present, she greeted old friends, talked briefly with people about different paintings and was pleased for Edgar that he had a good turnout.

Edgar appeared at her elbow in a gray suit with a pale blue tie that brought out the blue in his eyes. He looked his usual friendly self, as if their last conversation had never occurred.

"To anyone who doesn't know you, you look as if you're having a good time," he said. "To me, you look as if you're hurting. Sophia, you've made an appearance. You don't have to stay."

"I'm fine, Edgar. Thanks, though, for telling me I can go."

"Have you thought over what I said to you?"

"Of course."

"I won't ask your conclusions. Have you seen Garrett?"

"Not at all. I haven't talked to him or seen him this past week, which is what I told him I wanted. Whatever I do, Edgar, I do not intend to pursue a relationship with Garrett," she said, thinking her words sounded hollow and false to her own ears.

"That decision is solely yours and I have no comments to make. I don't usually interfere in your life."

"No, you don't, and I appreciate that as much as I appreciate the comments you make concerning my paintings and the art world."

"Good. We're getting another good turnout tonight."

"You are. The flowers are beautiful," she said, glancing around the room at baskets of flowers that held anniversary cards.

"Lots of people accepted my invitations and responded. We've sold two of your paintings and the evening is quite early."

"That's gratifying."

"Are you still going to Santa Fe?"

"Probably, but I haven't made arrangements yet."

"Good. I think you should stay here this time of year." He glanced around. "The crowd is growing. I'll go greet the new arrivals." He moved away and she walked along, greeting people she knew.

As she made her way through the gallery, she glanced toward the front door and her heart skipped. She looked into Garrett's gray eyes and it was as if they were alone in the gallery. All noise, surroundings, people—everything faded from her awareness except him.

Seven

Without breaking eye contact, Garrett walked through
the crowd toward her. In a dark suit and tie, he looked
as handsome as ever and every inch the part of the
wealthy, commanding executive. The closer he came,
the more her heart pounded. With an effort she looked
away, turning to gaze at a painting and keeping her
back to him.

Her emotions seesawed from joy at the very sight
of him to the familiar anger she had borne for nearly
a week.

"Sophia."

His deep voice sent electricity racing over her nerves.
She turned to face him.

"Why are you here?" she asked. In spite of her simmer-
ing anger, her voice held a softer tone she couldn't hide.

"I knew you'd be here. I received an invitation a
while back from Edgar."

"We have nothing to say," she said stiffly and turned her back. Garrett stayed beside her.

"I have something to say. Have you thought about our conversation?"

"Of course I have. I've thought constantly about all of it, about what you said and what you did."

"You can't blame the Delaneys for trying to meet you. All they ask is a chance to talk with you. Frankly, they're curious, too, about their half sister."

"I have no curiosity whatsoever about meeting them. Particularly if any of them would remind me of my father," she said, yet her words sounded hollow and empty. She clung to her old argument out of habit, but it was beginning to lose strength. Garrett had stepped in and changed her life.

"They'll all remind you of him, just as you'll remind them of him."

She shot him a look as anger welled up. "That wasn't what I wanted to hear."

"Sophia, let go of your grudges and just give them a chance. You can give yours away and after a year on the Delaney board, if you still feel the way you do now and don't like them, you can go on your way and never see them again. But if you give them a chance, I think you'll find a family that you will grow to love." He stepped closer and she turned away slightly.

"I sent you some brochures and annual reports. You'll see all the good the Delaney Foundation is doing. That all started when Will stepped in. Argus built that fortune, but Will and his brothers are the ones who have put Delaney money to many good uses. If you cooperate, more wealth can be poured into charitable causes, good causes that Argus never gave a dime to. That is sweet revenge right there, Sophia."

She looked up to meet his gaze.

"Spend Argus's money in a manner he never did," he urged.

Without commenting, she moved on to look at another grouping of pictures and was aware that Garrett followed, moving close beside her. She detected his aftershave, a scent that triggered unwanted, painful memories of being with him. Memories that tormented her.

"I'm glad you've thought about our conversation. If you change your mind, let me set up a meeting. I'll fly you to Dallas and back whenever you want. Or if you prefer, any or all of them will come to Houston and meet whenever and wherever you want."

"Garrett," she said, her voice so low it was almost a whisper. "If I decide to see them, I will not go through you. As I already said, I don't want to see you or talk to you again," she said. Even as the words left her mouth, she remembered Edgar's warning that she was letting go of a good man.

"Have you once thought about if our situations had been reversed? What would you have done?"

Startled again, she glanced up and looked away, clamping her jaw closed and refusing to answer.

"I didn't think so," he stated. "I didn't have to tell you who I work for or anything else when I did. I voluntarily told you when you knew nothing about it."

"That doesn't win you any points. I still feel deceived. I trusted you in the ultimate way, which I wish I could undo or at least forget."

A muscle worked in his jaw and his gray eyes seemed to consume her. Her pulse raced and even as she was lashing out at him because she hurt, she remembered his kisses too well.

"I'm sorry you feel that way. I don't. I can't forget

and I'd never want to undo the moments we spent together."

She should stop him or walk away—anything to reject him—but she couldn't move, trapped in his compelling gaze. His focus shifted to her mouth and she couldn't get her breath. In spite of her anger with him, there was no way to forget his kisses. She grew hotter with fury because she could not stop reacting to him physically.

Taking a deep breath, she turned away, breaking the mesmerizing spell. She moved on, no longer seeing him in her peripheral vision. Finally, she couldn't keep from looking. When she glanced around he was gone.

Her first reaction of disappointment stirred a surge of anger. She should be glad he had left. She tried to forget him, but it was impossible. Feeling unhappy and forlorn, she gathered her things and left without interrupting Edgar, who was talking to people.

At home, she sank in a chair. Her unhappiness grew, settling on her like a dense fog that shut out everything else. Garrett had looked so handsome tonight. She thought of being in his arms, the shared laughter and the passionate moments. She reminded herself that she was not in love with him, but she still felt betrayed. Impatiently, she changed clothes and went to her studio, pouring herself into her work, trying to shut out memories and longing. But once again, she had to stop because she was doing a poor job, ruining what had started as a satisfactory painting.

She spent the weekend in misery, with Garrett's arguments constantly nagging her. Everything he had said, Edgar had echoed. She had always tied the Delaney sons to their father, but they'd simply ended up with him, too, through no fault of their own, just as Garrett had pointed out.

Monday morning the brochures and reports Garrett had sent arrived in the mail. Clipped to the annual report was an envelope. She opened it to shake out the contents.

Snapshots fell on the table. She couldn't keep from looking at them as they tumbled out of the envelope and she saw the Delaney brothers. And there were pictures of the little girl, Caroline.

Sophia's insides clutched and she drew a deep breath. She picked up each picture, starting with one of Caroline. In a pink sundress, she had a huge smile and held a furry white dog in her arms. Sophia set aside the picture and picked up one of four men smiling at the camera. She recognized Will from the picture Garrett had showed her.

She stared at all of them. She bore the most resemblance to the two older brothers, Will and his deceased brother, Adam. For a while she pored over them before setting them aside and pulling out an annual report to start reading. A lot of money was going to help Dallas schools and parks, autistic children, medical research, various university scholarships. There was a long list.

Next, Sophia pulled out the will and read, seeing what would occur if they did not claim their legacies. It was a clear paragraph in which Argus stated that each inheritance would go to the church Argus attended and to the city for art projects—both worthy charities, but that money could do so much more if she cooperated with the Delaneys.

Rubbing her forehead, Sophia continued to think. When she considered meeting with them, should it be one or all of them? Would she feel overwhelmed by them? She could request they meet in Houston where she was at home. When the possibility began to overwhelm her, she went to her studio to inventory her paints and repair a broken chair, trying to think about something else, but she kept seeing the picture of Will and Caroline—the two people who looked the most like her.

Would it hurt to fly to Dallas and meet them? In spite of her anger with Garrett and what she had said to him, she imagined telling Garrett she would go with him. Even though she didn't want to go back to the relationship she'd had with Garrett, she knew she would feel better if he was with her.

She shook her head. She couldn't do it and she wanted to spend more time thinking about it.

In the late afternoon Edgar called to ask her to dinner.

"Thank you," she replied, smiling faintly. "But I don't want another lecture on why I should see the Delaneys. I think I'll pass, Edgar."

"Sophia, you and I go way back. I feel like a father to you. Whatever you decide, I do not want it to come between us."

"It won't as far as I'm concerned. But you may be unhappy with my decision."

"I'll live with whatever you decide. I really have your best interests at heart, though."

"I know you do," she replied with a sigh. "I've been giving it consideration today."

"Excellent news. Somehow I thought you would eventually let reason take charge. Usually you're quite levelheaded and sensible, and I expected the moment to come when you could stand back and see what you're doing here."

"Edgar, I'm getting the lecture again."

"All right, I apologize. If you don't want dinner, I'll try again another time. But don't go flying off to Santa Fe. Running isn't going to help on this one."

"All right, I'll bear your suggestion in mind."

"'Bye, Sophia."

She put away her phone and gazed into space. She didn't feel like eating. The sun slanted in the western sky and in another hour twilight fell. With it her spirits sank and nothing could get her mind off the Delaneys—and Garrett. She thought about the time she had spent with him, going back over their moments together, their lovemaking. Had he really cared about her? Or had it been a tactic he used while he tried to get close to her for his own purposes?

Even though his deception hurt badly, she missed him and his dynamic personality. Her life had been different with him, more exciting even through the most ordinary moments.

Have you once thought about if our situations had been reversed? What would you have done? His words had echoed continually in her memory. If she had been the one to try to get to know him with secret intentions, would she have had the same kind of reaction?

Had Edgar been right—was she making a mistake she would regret forever? Worse, had her anger with Garrett been misplaced? Had he been working toward a solution that would help them all, including her?

Garrett flew home Monday morning and went to see Will in the afternoon. Entering Will's office, Garrett carried a wrapped package under his arm. He crossed the room to place it on Will's desk.

"What's that?"

"It's for you, from me."

Will gave Garrett a puzzled, searching look and picked up the package to open it while Garrett settled in a leather chair across from the desk.

He tossed aside wrappings and paper and lifted out a painting in a simple wooden frame. "Garrett, this is excellent."

"It's one of hers. Now I don't have to tell you that she is truly talented—you can see for yourself."

"Damn, I'll say. This is a great picture. Looks like Santa Fe."

"It probably is."

"I'll put it here in the office. Give me a sales slip and you don't need to bear the expense."

"Forget it. It's a gift. Of course, she knows nothing about it."

"Yeah, too bad," Will said. His smile faded as he set the picture on a nearby table and then picked up the wrapping to dispose of it in the trash. He sat and faced Garrett.

"I did my best, Will. Sorry I didn't come back with Sophia."

"We all know you did what you could. What do you think? Any chance she'll appear?"

"I don't think there is, but she *was* taken aback when I showed her your picture with Caroline and told her this was Caroline's future inheritance, too."

"She must have really hated the old man. He didn't abuse any of us, he just ignored us until we were young adults. Even then, it was never a deep relationship. But once I started in this business that all changed."

"From what I could glean her anger toward him came mostly from him ignoring her. And she's angry over how much he hurt her mother. He merely liked her mother, but her mother always loved him."

"I don't know where we go from here."

"I'll think about it. In the meantime, keep hope alive because I sent her annual reports and brochures about the companies. I sent a few family pictures. I've said a lot to her that she can't keep from thinking about."

"Good. Maybe your efforts will pay off."

"It may be Caroline who does it."

"I don't care how it comes about, but we'd all like to know her. We'd like to have her in the family, which is where she belongs. Give her time and then you can try again."

"Next time, Will, get someone else. She's made it clear she doesn't want to deal with me."

"Garrett, sorry if this job assignment interfered—" Will started.

Garrett shook his head. "I'm ready to start catching up here. If you want me, I'll be in my office."

As Garrett stood, Will came to his feet. "Garrett, we all appreciate what you did for us. Time will tell. It may be too soon to judge."

"Even though she hasn't yielded on this, she's a great person. She's a very talented artist. I bought five paintings, including yours. I liked her."

"Evidently you had something going with her and this killed it. I'm sorry for that."

Garrett shrugged. "She was happy to tell me good-bye."

He walked out, feeling as if his story with Sophia was now officially over. He went back to his office in long strides and closed the door, crossing to his desk to start on the backlog of email. He only got through two before he stopped to pull out his phone and retrieve the picture of Sophia in the snow. His insides clenched as he looked at her picture. Memories engulfed him of that night and that moment when he could not resist kissing her.

He ached for her. Realizing where his thoughts were going, he put away his phone and concentrated on trying to catch up on work that had piled up while he had been away. But all through the day, memories of Sophia were distractions. His thoughts would drift to her and then when he realized he was lost in reminiscence and forgetting his work, he would try to focus.

Wednesday night, when he returned home from work, Garrett swam laps and worked out before going to his room to shower. As he dressed, he pulled on sweatpants and a sweatshirt. Glancing at a bedside table, he picked up the delicate gold bracelet he had given Sophia. He turned it in his hand, remembering it on her wrist. He recalled the moment she had thrown it at him. With a sigh, he laid it back on the table.

He wasn't hungry so he skipped dinner and went to his workshop to start building a rocking chair, sawing and losing himself in the labor, finding a respite from memories for a short time only to stop working to think about her.

He shook his head and returned to building the chair, a task that at any other time in his life would have given him real pleasure. But not now, not tonight.

Thursday came and he hadn't talked to Will about Sophia since Monday. She apparently had held to her original decisions and his disappointment was heavy. As he sat in his office, his cell phone beeped. He glanced at the number and frowned, growing nervous and curious. He touched it to say hello and heard Sophia's voice.

"Good morning," he said cautiously, hope flaring.

He struggled to keep from speculating on the reason for her call.

"You win, Garrett," she said, and he closed his eyes. Just her voice made his heart thud. He wanted to see her and be with her to such an extent it took a second for her message to register. His eyes flew open.

"How's that?" he asked, holding his breath.

"I've decided that I will meet with the Delaneys."

Relief swamped him, and along with it, his yearning to be with her intensified. "Sophia, you won't regret it," he said. "I'll arrange the meeting wherever you want."

There was silence and his heart drummed as she hesitated. "I'd like you to come with me. This is not something I expected to be doing and I don't want to meet them alone."

"Of course I'll go with you if that's what you want. How about Saturday evening for dinner, if that gives Zach time to get back from wherever he is?"

"Whatever you work out," she said in a quiet, forlorn voice that didn't sound like her. "I haven't decided what I'll do, but I will talk to them. I would prefer to avoid having attorneys present for this meeting. This is just to meet and get acquainted."

"That's all I asked. Then it will be between you and the Delaneys. I don't think you'll be sorry. You're doing the right thing—the unselfish thing."

"We'll see."

"You can stay at my house. We can keep out of each other's way. If that doesn't suit you, I know you can stay at Will's."

"I'll stay at your house," she replied, surprising him.

"Excellent. How about flying Saturday early afternoon?"

"That's fine."

"I'll pick you up at one. It'll take little more than an hour to get here."

"I know."

"Sophia, thanks," he said, meaning it, his heart racing with joy, relief and longing. He would see her in two days. "I'll be glad to see you."

"I'll see you Saturday," she said. Noncommittal words spoken in a noncommittal tone. Was she still angry? Or did staying with him mean she might give him another chance? He had no idea what to make of her tone or her plans. "My house at one."

"That's great. The Delaneys will be overjoyed that you've agreed to meet them. And, Sophia, I'll be glad to see you. I've missed you."

"We'll see each other Saturday," she said in the same noncommittal tone.

"I can't wait," he said. "See you soon."

"'Bye, Garrett."

She was gone. His pulse raced. He tried to curb his excitement because it was a baby step in the right direction, but not a commitment.

Saturday. Eagerness lifted his spirits.

He called Will on his cell. Before Will could even say hello, Garrett spoke. "I just had a call from Sophia, Will. I'm picking her up Saturday afternoon at one, and you all can meet with her Saturday night. I figured it would be easiest to do this over a dinner because it will be more relaxed than meeting in an office."

"You did it, Garrett!" Will exclaimed. "I knew you could. You got her to agree to meet with us. We couldn't get along without you. Thank you beyond words. I'll call Zach and Ryan and get them here. Saturday night we'll have dinner at my place. Fantastic, Garrett. Way to go. Talk to you later."

Will was gone and Garrett had to laugh and shake his head. He thought about Sophia and his laughter faded. He wanted more than just to see her, fly with her, go to Will's with her. Saturday night she would stay at his house. He couldn't wait to see her and wished he had asked if she wanted to come tonight. Saturday seemed far too distant in the future.

Eight

On the sunny Saturday afternoon, Sophia heard a car motor and looked out to see Garrett park in front and hurry to the front door. With a final touch of her hair that was tied back by a white scarf, she glanced briefly at her image. Her gaze ran over her white crepe dress and high-heeled white pumps,

When she opened the door, Garrett smiled. "Hi."

When Sophia told Garrett hello, her heart missed beats. She still had mixed feelings about what Garrett had done, about seeing the Delaneys, about accepting her legacy. But she had the same intense, instant reaction to him, stronger now than ever. She ached to be in his arms.

An uncustomary nervousness disturbed her over meeting the Delaney sons. She was glad to have Garrett at her side even though she continued to deal with her smoldering anger at his betrayal. However, she had to finally agree he was right. The Delaneys could not help who fathered them any more than she could. And she had never knowingly hurt anyone in her life the way she had been about to hurt all the Delaney principal heirs.

"I'm glad you agreed to come with me," she said quietly. "I don't expect to be in Dallas beyond this weekend, so I only have this bag."

"I'll carry it," he said, taking it from her to put it on his shoulder. His fingers brushed hers and a tingle sizzled through her. She continued to have the same volatile physical reactions to him, maybe more so because of being away from him.

He drove to the airport where they boarded a waiting private jet. Even though she was intensely aware of him beside her, she sat quietly looking out the window below at a long bayou lined on one side by tall pines. When they were at cruising altitude, she turned to find him watching her.

"You're doing the right thing."

"I suppose, Garrett. I'm nervous about it," she admitted, looking into his fascinating gray eyes. In spite of all that had happened, she still thought he would be incredibly interesting as a subject for a portrait. She had to struggle to keep her mind from imaging what it would be like to paint him, how intimate it would be...

"Why?" he asked, his eyes widening. "There's no earthly reason for you to be nervous."

"I suppose it's another carryover from childhood. My father also intimidated me. If and when he paid any attention to me, he would fire questions at me about how I was doing in school. I never seemed to give him the right answer."

A faint smile played on Garrett's face. "Argus Delaney could be intimidating. I know what you're talking about—I was grilled in the same manner. 'What are your grades this semester, Garrett? Why did you just make a 98 on a test instead of a perfect score? Your dad tells me you don't want to take a third year of Latin. Why not?'" Garrett said, imitating her father in what seemed an accurate portrayal. She had to smile.

"You sound the way I remember him. Didn't your dad work for him?"

"Oh, yes. So why did Argus quiz me about grades? He took an interest in my dad, therefore he took an interest in my life. My dad was happy to have Argus on my case as well as himself, so I was caught between the two of them, which I viewed as totally unfair. My dad never quizzed Will or gave him a hard time and I resented Argus for working me over when I wasn't his son."

"That sounds like him," she said, finding it difficult to imagine the commanding, decisive man seated by her as a boy who was intimidated by the same man she had been. "Was he hard on his sons?"

"Yes. If he was around. Frankly, a good deal of the years they were young, he probably ignored them as much as he did you. They went to boarding schools and Argus traveled."

"Yes, to see us," she said bitterly.

"Usually, Argus wasn't a lovable man—an exception was your mother. Maybe with women he was lovable, but in his other relationships, I doubt it. Intimidating, domineering, he got people to do what he wanted them to do."

"Are any of his sons like him in that manner? If so, it would have been better to bring my attorney to this meeting."

"I don't see it, but I've grown up knowing all of them. Will is my age, Zach and Ryan are younger. Will is as kind as can be with Caroline. She had a lot of problems after her father died. She shut herself off in her own world. She wouldn't talk to anyone. Will tried everything he could think of—doctors, counselors, tutors. Finally, he found a teacher who got through to Caroline and she opened up and became the child she was when her father was alive. Then Will married the teacher."

"Caroline looked like a happy little girl in the picture you showed me."

"She is now."

"I suppose I expected all three sons to be like Argus and my reaction to them to be the same. And I wasn't looking forward to encountering three carbon copies of my father."

"You won't, I can promise. The Delaney brothers are charming and delighted to meet you. They'll be as nice as they can be to you."

"My mother always said my father could be charming. I never saw that side to him."

"You'll see it in Will and that's what his dad was when he wanted to be. Frankly, I never found Argus to be charming. I was raised to call him Uncle Argus. I was quite delighted to learn that he was not my true uncle and that that was merely a title of respect. I didn't want to be related to him, probably any more than you."

"You surprise me. I wouldn't have guessed. If I had known that from the first—"

She broke off, remembering she had had no clue that Garrett had known her father, and that Garrett had had no intention of telling her.

"Do you understand yet why I did what I did?" he asked quietly.

"I suppose I do, because I wouldn't have seen you if you had told me you were sent by my half brothers," she said, looking into his gray eyes and trying to ignore the current of desire that simmered steadily. In spite of the division between them, she found him as appealing and sexy as ever. She had missed him and didn't want to look too intently at how strong her feelings ran for him. She was forgiving him easily, the same way her mother had always excused Argus and forgiven him. She was falling into the same trap her mother had, doing everything her mother had done—having an affair, forgiving the man, losing her heart to him no matter how he treated her. A chill ran down her spine. She was doing all the same things. Would she end up in the same situation as her mother—or worse?

He leaned close and she felt as if she were drowning in depths of misty gray. His fingers brushed her cheek. Tingles spun outward from the contact while she felt consumed in his direct study. She wondered whether he could hear her drumming pulse.

"Do you forgive me, Sophia?"

Her heart lurched. How easy it would be to say yes and go back to where they were before, but she couldn't do it. "Maybe. It isn't quite the same yet. That hurt, Garrett." The words came out sounding more sharp than she intended. Yearning showed in the depths of his eyes, stirring too many vivid memories.

Watching her, he slowly leaned closer. She couldn't get her breath. Her lips parted and her heart thudded. Garrett's gaze drifted down to her mouth, heightening her longing. He had to hear her heart pounding. He placed one hand on her knee and his other hand went behind her head to hold her as he continued to lean closer.

She could back off, tell him no, move away, refuse him. Instead, she leaned forward and closed her eyes.

His mouth covered hers, opening hers wider to give him access. He pulled her closer while her heart slammed against her ribs. Blazing with a need for so much more of him, she couldn't help but kiss him in return.

"When we get off this plane—" he whispered.

She shook her head. "I didn't intend for that to happen," she said. "Slow down. You're still going too fast."

"I missed you," he said. "Stay over longer to go out with me, even if it's only one evening."

She inhaled deeply, knowing she shouldn't while at the same time wanting to more than anything else.

"Sophia, I did what I had to. And it will give you an inheritance worth several billion dollars. That's not the same as deceiving you to hurt you. If you go through with this, you'll give the Delaney brothers what they want and set up money for Caroline so she will never have a worry. You saw the charities and how much they've given. So this is different—vastly different from deceiving you to do something underhanded or hurtful. I know you can see the difference whether you admit it or not."

"All right, Garrett, I can. It doesn't stop me from feeling deceived, or feeling my trust in you has been betrayed."

Her gaze lowered again to his mouth and she thought of his kisses. Her heart started pounding once more. She wanted to kiss him while at the same time she didn't want to see him again—it was confusing, overwhelming. With a deep breath, she leaned back.

"Garrett, we better stop this and get on a less personal note for now."

"I know what I want, Sophia. I want you in my arms and I want to make love to you again," he stated in a husky voice that made her shiver with anticipation. His gray eyes conveyed his desire, holding her mesmerized as he could so easily do. "We *will* make love again."

"You're so confident," she said.

He unbuckled his seat belt to lean forward and kiss her again, a hard, possessive kiss that made her heart pound until she longed to be alone with him. She ran her hands across his broad shoulders while she moaned softly.

He stopped abruptly and she opened her eyes to find him watching her with desire and satisfaction both clearly in his expression.

"I'm going to love you, Sophia. We'll finish what we've started."

She looked away, thinking about all that had happened between them. He was buckled back into his seat when she turned back. "Garrett, nothing has changed about my feelings concerning an affair and you have clearly convinced me you will not consider marriage for years. I don't want a casual affair. We had a night of passion. That's all. I will not get into a relationship like my mother had. You may have forgotten what I told you."

"I haven't forgotten," he said.

She looked outside again, her emotions stormy. She wanted him, wanted his loving, wanted to make love with him in every way, yet she still harbored anger over what he had done. She wondered if he thought her turnaround about the Delaneys meant she had changed her attitude about an affair with him, but she had not.

"How is the painting going?" he asked as if they had been separated months instead of days.

"I'm as busy as ever," she said. "How's the furniture?"

He smiled. "I've started a chair. Building something relieves tension. I'm enjoying the paintings I bought. They remind me of you."

"I'm glad. When I return home, I'm going to Santa Fe." He nodded. After a moment of silence, she said, "I told Edgar about this meeting and he was pleased. He agrees with you about this whole thing and he has my best interests at heart."

"I know he does."

"He's sort of a tie with my mom even though she's gone. Edgar is the father I wished I'd had in some ways."

"Remember, Sophia, this meeting isn't about Argus. It's about you and your brothers and the future."

"I've studied the Delaneys' pictures so I'll know which one is which."

"You won't have any difficulty with that. You'll know Will at once."

"Tell me about them again, please."

"With Adam gone, Will is the oldest surviving brother. He's always acted the oldest anyway. He's a decisive, take-charge person. Zach is forthright, practical, but at the same time, he's a renegade, the wanderer who never settles. Ryan is the youngest, outgoing, enthusiastic, an optimist, a cowboy at heart."

"They don't sound formidable when you talk about them. I'm so nervous about this, Garrett."

"Don't be. They're nice guys and they're going to like you. They're still in shock to discover a half sister."

"How could he have kept my mother and me from them all these years? Especially after they were grown."

"I don't think any of them were keenly interested in where he spent all his time as long as he stayed out of their lives and wasn't meddling. He's one of the reasons all of them have been so leery of marriage. The divorce was ugly. They fought and it upset his sons. Later, Adam married and she walked out early on. She was a party person. She wasn't interested in Caroline. It helped build a strong case against marriage."

"You said all that has had an influence on you."

"I guess it has. People change, though. Will fell in love and married, and he seems happier than I've ever seen him. Ava is great and so good with Caroline."

The pilot announced the descent into Love Field in Dallas. Sophia couldn't keep her nerves calm. Three half brothers she had never met. Argus's family. Garrett had been reassuring, but they were still Delaneys. Too clearly she could remember cold snubs or cutting remarks from her father.

Chilled, dreading the meeting in spite of Garrett's reassurances, she looked at Dallas spread out below. The sprawling city had long gray ribbons of freeways cutting through town. The aqua backyard pools were bright jewels set in green. Garrett's home was down there. All the Delaneys were there, waiting to meet her.

She was quiet on the ride to Garrett's home even though he kept up a cheerful running conversation. She suspected he was trying to put her at ease and he was succeeding to a certain extent.

As in Houston, they passed through a gated area and a gatekeeper waved. They wound up a long drive surrounded by oaks. When the mansion came into view, she was startled by his colossal home. "You're in a palace here," she said. "This is far more palatial than your Houston home."

"I spend a lot more time here," he said. "I'm in Houston only occasionally. This is where I call home."

"It's magnificent," she said, her gaze roaming over tile roofs above a mansion that had wings spreading on both sides and angling around out of her sight. A formal pond with three tiered fountains was flanked by tall oaks. "This is beautiful, Garrett. Far too fancy for my paintings here."

"Oh, no. I already have one of your paintings hanging here."

"When did you do that?"

"Earlier this week when I came back from Houston."

"You've been back here? Where were you when I called you to tell you that I would talk to the Delaneys?" she asked, realizing for the first time that he might have flown from Dallas to get her.

"I was in Dallas," he replied with a faint smile.

"Why didn't you tell me? I could have flown to Dallas by myself."

"This was infinitely more fun. I wanted to see you again and be with you." He picked up her hand to run his thumb over her knuckles. "I wanted to kiss you and hold you again. I was more than happy to fly to Houston and ride back with you."

"Thank you," she said, smiling and shaking her head. "When I called your cell phone, I never thought about you being in Dallas."

"I know you didn't and that's fine," he said as he parked at the front door. "Leave your bag. I'll get someone to bring it in," he said as he climbed out and came around.

At the top of wide steps they crossed a porch with a huge crystal-and-brass light hanging overhead. One of the massive twelve-foot double doors opened before they reached it and a man stepped out, smiling as he greeted them.

"Sophia, this is Roger, who has worked for my family for over thirty years now. Roger, this is Miss Delaney. She has a bag in the car."

"Yes, sir. Welcome to the house, Miss Delaney," he said.

"Thank you," Sophia replied as she entered a wide hallway with a staircase winding to the second floor and a twenty-foot ceiling.

"Garrett, Roger is older," she said. "I can get my bag or you can—"

"Forget it, Sophia. Roger works out every day. I've played tennis with him since I was a kid and I still can't beat him. If you saw him lift weights, you wouldn't be concerned. He worked for my folks and now he works for me. Actually, he's more like a relative to me than an employee. I grew up knowing him, which makes the relationship different from just employer and employee."

"That's nice, Garrett," she said, seeing another facet to Garrett in his relationships with the people in his life.

"I'll show you your room so you can change for dinner," he said while they climbed the stairs to the second floor and walked down a wide hall. They entered another wing. He continued, finally motioning toward an open door. She entered a beautiful suite with ornate fruitwood furniture.

"I hope I can find my way back where we came from."

"You will, and my room is down the hall. I won't let you get lost."

"Do you really live here alone?"

"On this floor. Roger has a large suite of rooms on the third floor. So does my chef, Larrier. There are two more suites where Andrea and Dena live. They're in charge of the cleaning crew. They have another entrance to that wing and we can all avoid getting in each other's way. There's an elevator farther along the main hall. I have a finished attic above the third level where luggage and various items are stored. I can give you a tour tomorrow."

She laughed. "Show me your studio and your furniture, but skip the tour. This place is far too big."

"Is there anything you need?"

"No, thank you."

He crossed the room to her to untie the ribbon holding her hair. She shook her head and her hair swung over her shoulders. Her pulse drummed now that she stood so close to him. She looked up at him, reminded again of how tall he was.

"Garrett, I can't keep from being nervous about this. The whole thing seems weird. I was six when my father divorced their mother. If he had married my mother then, as she wanted him to, I would have suddenly had four brothers. I would have grown up with them. Now I'm finally going to meet them. Suppose they don't like me?"

"They're going to love you. Are you kidding? Sophia, you're the key to them each inheriting four billion dollars. That will make them love anything you do."

"When you put it that way, it sounds ridiculous for me to worry. Also, it sounds as if money is the most important thing in their lives."

"It's not, I promise you. But what is this? You are so cool and poised in the art world and you're falling apart here?"

"This is entirely different. I've never had a close family except Mom. To suddenly know I'll be face-to-face with half brothers gives me the jitters."

"You can relax. Forget your father. His sons are very

nice guys. Ava is wonderful and Caroline is a little doll. The Delaneys are blood relatives, Sophia. You'll find they're like you."

She inhaled deeply as she gazed into Garrett's eyes. His words reassured her, but now that Garrett stood close and rested one hand casually on her shoulder, her attention shifted to him and she forgot her concerns about the Delaneys. Her nervousness vanished, replaced by awareness of Garrett and growing desire.

"Thanks for coming to get me and for sticking with me tonight."

"I missed you," he said solemnly and she could only nod. He slipped his hand in his pocket and picked up her wrist, turning her palm up. He placed the gold bracelet in her hand. "I want you to have this. Will you take it back?"

She looked down at the fine filigree gold in her hand before closing her fingers over it and looking back up at him. Her answer would mean forgiveness. She hesitated another second, knowing the path she was taking.

"Yes, I want it. Thank you, Garrett," she said. She was letting him back in her life and that would cause a whole different set of problems.

He slid his arm around her waist and pulled her to him as he leaned down to kiss her.

The instant his mouth touched hers, passion burst into flames. It was as if they had never been apart or had any angry words between them. Wrapping her arms around him, she clung tightly, kissing him with a fierce hunger.

While her heart pounded, she lost awareness of anything except Garrett, wanting him with all her being, holding him as if she feared losing him again. She let go of her anger and let her pent-up longing surface.

His hand drifted over her, sliding down her back and over her bottom, drifting up to her nape to caress her until she stopped him.

"Garrett, I need to get ready for tonight," she said, gasping for breath.

He looked at her a long moment and then he turned to go. "I'll come get you here when I'm ready." She nodded, watching as he walked out and closed the door behind him.

She turned to look at the elegant sitting room that looked like a formal living room. The floors were polished oak with furniture that looked antique, each piece a gem. She strolled to the bedroom, which was a beautiful room with a king-size canopied bed.

Turning her bracelet, she thought about Garrett. She could no longer deny it— She had fallen in love with him. She had never before felt this way about someone. No other man had ever been as important to her.

I'm not ready to get tied down. She could remember his words clearly yet it was impossible to resist Garrett. The struggle was growing. The more she wanted him, the more important commitment became.

She pulled off her sweater and gathered her things to head for the shower, hoping to clear her head before tonight.

When Garrett rapped lightly on her door, she was dressed and ready. Trying to be conservative, she wore a plain black dress with a high neck and long sleeves. The dress ended above her knees and she wore high-heeled black pumps. Her hands were cold and some of her nervousness had returned. She crossed the room to open the door, catching her breath at the sight of him in an open-necked shirt, a charcoal sports jacket and gray trousers.

When Garrett smiled, her nervousness dropped slightly. As his gaze took a slow inventory, his expression revealed his approval. "You're beautiful," he said.

"Thank you," she replied, feeling slightly better again.

"Shall we go?"

"If we have to," she answered.

"Stop worrying. You'll see."

"I hope you're right."

During the drive on the chilly fall night, Garrett kept up the cheerful chatter again. They didn't have far to go and soon she found herself at another palatial estate with lights ablaze and a party atmosphere already in the air.

Inside they were shown to a reception room that she barely noticed. Across the room stood a brown-eyed man with thick, wavy black hair. Handsome, he was slightly shorter than Garrett. Even she could see a family resemblance, realizing if she had seen him in a crowd on the street, she would have looked twice because he had the same bone structure she had, the same eyes.

As he smiled and crossed the room to her, she extended her hand. He accepted it, his hand closing around hers in a firm clasp. "Welcome to the Delaney family," he said and hugged her lightly. He released her and continued to smile. "We're strangers in a way, but one look at you and I know you're my sister. And we're not going to be strangers ever again. We're family."

"Thank you, William," she said, her nervousness and concern evaporating because he was as welcoming as Garrett said he would be.

"Please, call me Will. Everyone is coming, but I

wanted to meet you first. Sophia, thank you for meeting with us and giving us a chance here. I have to admit, we're all curious about our newly discovered sister. Unfortunately, we knew absolutely nothing about your existence. My dad kept things to himself."

"I didn't know that none of you knew about me, because I've always known about you. I never saw any pictures, though."

"That's enough about him. I want you to meet the family. They're waiting for us. One more thing—don't blame Garrett for what happened in Houston because we really pressured him. He's like a brother to all of us and we took advantage of that."

"I'll remember," she said, glancing at Garrett, wondering if she had been far too harsh with him.

"Everyone is in the family room," Will said, taking her arm lightly. "I'll show you."

They walked past various large rooms and then Will entered an open area with Corinthian columns and a glass wall giving a view of the veranda and pool area. Two handsome men stood talking to a tall, slender, sandy-haired blonde. To one side a little girl with black curly hair sat playing with a small brown bear. She glanced at Sophia and looked down quickly at her bear. She was even prettier than her picture had been.

Will introduced Sophia first to his wife, Ava, and they shook hands briefly. Ava had a welcoming smile as she greeted her. "We're all so happy to meet you."

"This is something I never expected to be doing," Sophia admitted.

"They've been eager to meet you," Ava said, smiling at Will. Sophia felt the current that passed between Ava and Will, realizing they were deeply in love. She ignored the twinge of longing she felt as she observed them.

Will turned to Sophia. "Ava, excuse us and I'll continue introducing Sophia."

"Of course," she said, giving Sophia's hand a squeeze. "We'll talk later. I've never met a famous artist before."

Sophia smiled, instantly relaxing a degree as she shook her head. "I don't know about fame," she said. "But thanks, Ava," she added, more for being nice than what she had said.

Will steered Sophia to the child. Caroline's brown eyes were filled with curiosity as she gazed at Sophia, who smiled.

"Sophia, this is Caroline," Will said. "I know you've heard about her. Caroline, meet your aunt Sophia Rivers."

"How do you do, Caroline," Sophia said, smiling at her. "You look very pretty, Caroline. How old are you?"

"I'm five."

"Is that your favorite bear?"

Caroline nodded. "Yes, ma'am," she answered, hugging the bear.

"I guess you sleep with your bear."

"Yes, ma'am," Caroline said, smiling at her.

"And you have a dog, don't you?"

"I have Muffy."

"I've seen your picture with Muffy who is a very cute dog. Sometime I'll meet Muffy, too."

Caroline nodded.

"Caroline looks like you," Will said. "Excuse us, Caroline, while I introduce your aunt Sophia to your other uncles."

They crossed the room. "Garrett showed me pictures

of all of you. Let me guess," she said, standing in front of the two remaining Delaney brothers. "You must be Zach," she said, extending her hand to a curly-haired man with startling crystal-blue eyes that were so unlike the rest of the brown-eyed family.

"The brother who does not look like a brother," she said. "I'm glad to meet you."

"It's about time. Welcome to the Delaney family."

"Thank you," she said, turning to the youngest brother, another handsome man with brown hair. "You have to be Ryan."

"Indeed, I am. Thanks for coming to meet us. We've looked forward to this since the moment the attorney read Dad's will. Let me get you something to drink. We have everything from beer to champagne to cocktails—whatever suits you."

"I'd love a piña colada," she said.

Garrett appeared at her elbow. "Zach, bring me a martini, would you?"

In a short time, Sophia felt drawn to all of them. They shared stories of childhood, which she guessed were being told for her benefit. They were at their best, she was certain. All of them were entertaining, polite, friendly. Garrett was relaxed and happy here with his lifelong friends.

It was almost eleven when she saw an opportunity to change the subject of the conversation. "I really should go soon, but before I leave I want to say something while I'm with all of you." She glanced at Garrett who gave her a faint smile.

"I'm thrilled to meet my half brothers and relieved that you've welcomed me into the family. I'm happy to discover that I like all of you," she said with a nervous laugh. "Even though he was very good to my mother,

I did not have a satisfactory relationship with your father. In financial matters, he was generous, I will give him that. But that's the past and really has little to do with the current situation. I know your legacies hinge on me accepting my inheritance. Well, after meeting all of you, I'm happy to cooperate with all of you."

She was drowned out by thanks and cheers.

"We really appreciate this, Sophia," Will said.

"I blamed all of you for things that none of you did or had any control over, and it was wrong. I'm sorry, but this should make up for it."

"Don't give all that another thought," Zach said, smiling at her. "We're glad to know you. We all had our problems with our dad, so we understand a bit about how you feel. We just say a giant thank-you for doing this."

"I stand to benefit, too, in a very big way," she said, smiling. "The most important thing is that I'm not alone any longer. I feel I have a family now. Thanks to each of you for being so nice and welcoming me. I'm really overwhelmed and owe you an apology for being so uncooperative." She was quickly drowned out by them telling her to forget the past.

She felt a knot in her throat. They were being incredibly nice to her and she hated to think how cold she had been to them, and how angry she'd been with Garrett when he had tried to get her to see their side.

"I think it's time I go home before I get really emotional over all this. The evening has been delightful."

The goodbyes were long and it was almost midnight before she was in the car with Garrett. He reached over to squeeze her hand. "You were fantastic tonight and you did the right thing, Sophia."

"You were right, Garrett. They were all charming.

Ava made me feel as if I've known her a long time and Caroline is an adorable little girl. It's hard to imagine her going through all she has."

"Ava has been the biggest blessing for Caroline and probably for Will, too."

"I had a wonderful time. I know they were at their best, trying every way possible to please me. Well, they succeeded. That was the most delightful dinner party I've ever attended."

"You know you can keep part of your money and do so many things you want to do—the house and gallery in Santa Fe, the gallery in Taos."

"I have my own money. The Delaney money will go to charities."

"You'll make a lot of people incredibly happy."

At his house, he walked in with his arm across her shoulders. "Sophia," he said in a husky voice that made her pulse jump before they'd barely closed the door.

Nine

As she wrapped her arms around him, her heart pounded. Longing swamped her, making her tremble while his kiss melted her. She clung to him tightly, yielding to mindless loving, swept away by desire.

He wound his fingers in her hair and tipped her head back. "I missed you and have dreamed about you, thought about you, wanted you constantly. Forgive me."

"Garrett, I do. I shouldn't have been so harsh—thank heavens you made me see that."

"Sophia, will you trust me again?" he asked. She gave him a searching look and slowly nodded.

"I missed you," he repeated.

"We haven't been apart that long, Garrett," she whispered, his words making her heart beat even faster. His gray eyes were dark, stormy with passion. He had faint stubble now on his jaw and his hair was in disarray on his forehead. Her gaze lowered to his mouth and she wanted to kiss him. She pulled his head down and his lips covered hers, hard and demanding. Her pulse thundered, shutting out other sounds.

She had missed him dreadfully, more than she had wanted to admit to herself. Now she was desperate to love and be loved, to kiss and caress him once again.

He drew the zipper down the back of her dress. As cool air rushed over her shoulders, she felt his hands moving on her. He peeled away the dress and it fell in a whisper around her ankles. She kicked off her shoes and he held her back to look at her.

"You're so beautiful," he whispered while she tugged free his buttons and pushed his shirt off.

His hands drifted over her. When her lace bra fell, he cupped her breasts, his hands warm, his fingers a torment.

Wanting to get rid of any barriers between them, she unfastened his belt and then his trousers, shoving them off. In seconds she was in his arms, naked, warm, feeling his solid, hard body. While he kissed her, he picked her up to carry her to a bedroom. She was not conscious of where he took her—just that he placed her on a bed, kneeling to shower kisses on her while he drank in the sight of her and caressed her.

She moaned and pleasure heightened until it was torment for her. She rolled over to kiss him, knowing that she did love him.

He rolled her gently on her stomach and knelt to continue trailing kisses on her legs as she writhed and whispered endearments. When he reached her back, she rolled over, reaching for him. He stepped away to get protection and then returned, ready.

Kneeling between her legs, he lowered himself to enter her. Crying out his name, she wrapped her legs around him. She held him tightly, turning her head to kiss him and he filled her and withdrew, moving slowly, a tantalizing loving that heightened her need.

Writhing with passion, she clung to him as she cried out. "Love me, Garrett," she gasped. "Love me now."

"You are fabulous, perfect," he whispered in her ear as he slowly filled her again. Trying to pleasure her, his control stretched. Sweat beaded his shoulders and chest. Finally his control went and he pumped furiously as she moved with him.

He shuddered with release when his climax came and she thrashed wildly, soaring over a brink, caught up in rapture. "Garrett," she cried, clinging to him, unaware of anything beyond his body and hers together.

She held him tightly as they slowed, finally growing quiet. Keeping her close, he rolled on his side.

"I want you in my arms every night."

"That's impossible."

"It's not." He kissed her with light, feathery kisses on her temple, her cheek, down to her throat, lower until she stopped him.

"Just hold me, Garrett. I want you close."

"I want to hold you constantly, to kiss you, to love you," he said, kissing her between words. "What I'd like right now is for you to agree to go back to Colorado with me again next weekend."

"Garrett, I don't want to think about schedules or weekends or anything else right now except you."

"Good enough. We'll put the Colorado discussion off until later. Want to go for a midnight swim? The pool is heated."

"I don't have the energy and I'm surprised you do," she said, laughing.

"How about a hot bath instead? Just sit and soak and hold each other."

"That sounds far more interesting." He led her to a bathroom with a large marble tub.

"Where are we? Are we in your room?"

"No. This is a downstairs guest bedroom. I didn't carry you up a long flight of stairs, if you remember."

"I don't remember. You could have been carrying me outside to the car and I wouldn't have noticed, which means your loving takes all my attention."

"That's good news." He ran water, taking her hand to walk down three steps into the bath. Hot water swirled around her, but she was barely aware of it. All of her attention was on Garrett and his marvelous body with muscles from shoulders to feet.

As the tub filled, she sat between Garrett's legs, pressed against his wet, warm body while he wrapped his arms around her and held her. Another weekend in Colorado with him tempted her—it was something she would love to do—but it went against her good judgment.

Everything was different now. Because she was in love.

Hours later Garrett stirred. Dawn's pale light filtered into the room. He turned his head to look at Sophia who was in his arms, her legs entangled with his. Soft and warm, she took his breath away.

His gaze roamed slowly over her, memorizing her features. She excited him more than any other woman he had known. He wanted her with him—the extent of how badly surprised him. His feelings for her had grown over the weekend. He had missed her when they had been separated, but now he didn't want her to go back to Houston. He wanted her to stay with him.

He had never asked a woman to move in with him, but he wanted Sophia to do so. He ran his fingers through her hair, remembering her stating vehemently that she never wanted an affair. He brushed aside her declaration because they were past that now. She had seemed as eager as he to make love.

He mulled over asking her to move in—a commitment of sorts that he'd never given anyone before Sophia. But the thought of her flying back to Houston and then to Santa Fe and being unavailable for long periods was unacceptable.

It had been far worse than he had expected when she had been out of his life. Which raised a very important question: Was he falling in love with her?

He couldn't answer that. His usual caution and weighing of pros and cons kicked in from a lifelong habit of thinking things through before he acted.

He kissed her so lightly, dropping feathery kisses over her face, finally kissing her on her mouth. Then he lay back beside her, staring into space while he thought about asking her to stay.

When Sophia awoke, sunlight streamed through the windows. She turned to find Garrett smiling at her as he drew her to him.

"I'll cook your breakfast. Are you hungry?"

"Yes. I'll guess it's afternoon?"

"Good guess. I can see my watch," he said, turning to look at his watch on a bedside table. "It's almost one. Explains why I thought of food. Let's go shower and then I'll cook."

"If we shower together, which I think is what you're suggesting, then you won't be cooking for a while," she said, smiling at him. He smiled in return, turning back to kiss her.

"You might be right. Let's try and see," he said, stepping out of bed, picking her up to carry her to the shower. "I don't want to let go of you."

"That's fine with me," she replied. She wished he meant exactly what he said to her. She had fallen in love with him and she wanted his love—his commitment—in return. She felt shut away in their own tiny corner of paradise, yet too soon the world would intrude on them.

He set her on her feet in the shower and turned on the water. He slipped his arm around her waist and pulled her to him. His body was hard, muscled, warm and wet against hers. He bent his head to kiss her and all conversation ended.

Over an hour later they were back in bed in each other's arms. "I told you so, about showering together."

"So you're one of those people who has to say, 'I told you so.'"

"I am in this case."

"You must be hungry."

"Sort of," she replied. "Maybe I should shower on my own."

"Nope. No fun at all. Let's just try again. At some point our hunger might overcome our lust."

She laughed as she stepped out of bed. They showered and he gave her a navy robe to wear. He pulled on jeans and they went to a large kitchen with an adjoining dining area on one side and a living area on another. The house was as elegant inside as outside.

"Your house is beautiful."

"Thanks. I enjoy it. I had it built five years ago."

"Five years—you were young to have a house like this."

He shrugged. "I was fortunate and then I stepped into a job with the Delaneys."

She watched him work, thinking about his past and how neither the Delaneys nor Garrett had even known she existed. "What can I do to help?" she asked.

"You can sit there on a barstool and talk to me. Want coffee? Orange juice? What would you like?"

Barely aware of the answer she gave, she watched him as he moved around, getting eggs and toast. He was shirtless, his chest covered with dark curls. His muscles rippled as he moved and desire ignited again in her.

Instead of yielding to it, she tried restraint, chatting with him while erotic images flashed in her mind.

After breakfast he took her hand. "Let me show you my shop."

They walked to another wing where he entered a workshop much larger than the one he had in his Houston home. There was a wide, overhead door and pieces of wood scattered around with tools on the wall and in cabinets.

"I assume the overhead door leads to a drive, so you can get furniture in and out?"

"Mostly out. You're right."

She walked over to look at pieces on the table. "Looks as if you're starting something."

"I am. It's a rocker for you. I hope you like to rock."

Surprised, she glanced at him. "You're building that for me? You must have expected to see me again— expected us to get back together. A rocker is a big project," she said, suddenly wondering how much he wanted her in his life. To build a piece of furniture took time and effort. Was Garrett falling in love with her?

"Building something for you made me feel closer to you and gave me hope that we'd be together again."

She walked to him to put her arms around him. "I'll love it. I don't know what to say. It's wonderful, Garrett."

"Wait until it's finished. You might not even like it."

"Now you have to let me paint your picture."

He laughed and shook his head. "That one—I can't imagine why you'd want to. Would I hang for sale in a gallery somewhere?"

"Never. Let me take your picture and I can paint from that. Oh, wait—I have one of you already from Colorado."

"If painting my picture gives you pleasure, then by all means, go ahead. You're easy to please."

"Thank you," she said, smiling at him.

"I just wanted you to see my studio. Now's a good time for a swim."

"I don't have a suit."

"You don't need a suit," he said, his gray eyes holding obvious lust.

"You don't live alone," she said, pointing upstairs. "You told me about all the staff who live here."

He shook his head. "Forget it. They are in another wing and we're locked away unless I let them know I'm here and need them. When I do need them, I give them as much advance notice as possible."

"That works, but if we swim without suits, I don't think we'll ever get in the pool," she said.

"I think you might be right," he said, picking her up and kissing her. She wound her arms around his neck and returned his kisses as he carried her back to bed.

* * *

Late Sunday afternoon she was in his arms in his king bed in the upstairs bedroom. He showered kisses on her. "This is paradise, Sophia."

"I agree," she murmured, combing her fingers through locks of his unruly hair. "Your hair has a mind of its own."

"I learned that at a very early age."

"I love it this way. It keeps you from looking so much the executive and in charge and more like someone approachable and fun."

He chuckled and wrapped his fingers in her hair. "And I love your hair loose. It's sexy and gorgeous and makes you look enticing." As she said thank you, he raised on an elbow to look at her.

"I don't want you to go back to Houston today."

"I have to. I planned on it and I have an appointment tomorrow. I'm painting a portrait."

"I can't talk you into breaking that appointment?"

"Sorry, I need to keep it."

He toyed with her hair and studied her. "Sophia, stay with me. Move in with me. I'll build you a studio and you can fly to Houston or Santa Fe or anywhere else anytime you want. You can open a gallery here in Dallas. A gallery should do as well in Dallas as in Houston."

Her eyes widened and her heart drummed. A part of her wanted to say yes. If she moved in, would he eventually love her enough to want to marry her?

He was quiet, patiently waiting while his gaze was intently focused on her. His gray eyes were unfathomable and she had no idea what he really was thinking.

She sat up, pulling the sheet to her chin and turning to face him. "Garrett, I've talked about this with you from the very beginning. I've told you I do not want to have an affair."

"What do you think we're doing now?" he asked. "But what I'm suggesting would be a whole lot better."

"I'm flying home shortly and I'll go to Santa Fe. We can see each other and go out, but we're not living together. Maybe we'll have occasional weekends together, but nothing intense. Not weeks at a time. I'm keeping my independence and hopefully, my heart intact. I'll not spend my life sitting around getting bits and pieces of a man. We each make our choices," she said, hurting as she said the words. "I want to be with you and you know I do. I haven't been able to resist you. But I need to be on my own."

"You're damn scared to live," he said. "You compare everything with the past. I'm not Argus Delaney and I'd never treat you the way he did your mother. I want a relationship with you. I don't want this to end, and you sure as hell act like you're enjoying it."

"I am, but I want more of a commitment than moving in together." As soon as the words left her mouth, she almost couldn't believe she'd said them.

His eyes narrowed. Sitting up, he stared intently at her. "You want me to marry you."

"I know you don't want that kind of commitment. And I don't want anything less. If I marry, I'll want a family."

"Marriage might happen if we have a good relationship, but I'm not ready for that now. I want to know someone long and well before I make a lifetime commitment."

"I agree that's the best way," she said, her gaze roaming over his bare shoulders and chest. "I think we're at an impasse and I also think it's time to get ready to return to Houston."

"I've never asked anyone to move in with me, Sophia."

Her heart raced and she hurt at the same time. Contradictory emotions clashed. "I'm flattered and part of me wants to say yes and throw aside logic, but I'm not going to. I'm very pleased you told me this is a first invitation from you."

"This is a commitment of sorts."

"It sounds to me like you want a mistress instead of a wife."

"I've never thought of you in terms of a mistress. This is different."

"I can't really see how."

"Think about my offer, Sophia. Don't give me a flat no."

She gazed back, wanting to say yes but fighting her own desire. She had to get away before she gave in. She wanted more from him— She wanted his total commitment, his love.

He reached out to pull her into his arms. His possessive kiss and his hands moving over her, taking away the sheet easily, made her forget their conversation and everything else. She was in his arms and he was kissing her senseless and nothing else existed.

Moaning softly with pleasure, she ran her hands over his smooth, muscled back and was lost to loving him. He was in her arms now and she could pour out her love and try to capture his heart completely so he couldn't let her go.

It was early evening before they were airborne. They were quiet on the flight and she could feel the underlying tension between them. When they were finally at her door, she turned to him. "Want to come in?"

"Yes," he said, watching her unlock and open her door. They walked inside and Garrett closed her door, turning to face her.

"Would you like a drink?"

"What I'd like most of all is to hold you," he answered in a husky voice, pulling her into his embrace.

Just as earlier in the day, she forgot everything else. But this time there was a running hurt that nagged. Because of her rejection, she suspected she was losing him and that he would soon go out of her life for good. She threw herself into loving him, feeling that their times together were numbered.

He stayed the night and she lay in his arms as he slept. She wanted more nights with him, more times for each of them to fall deeply in love. She already was wildly in love with him. Was she making a huge mistake by letting him go? She had almost made a huge mistake in refusing to talk to the Delaneys. Was she doing the same kind of thing here—only more disastrous?

She could imagine living with Garrett, hoping for a proposal, feeling the insecurity of an affair. She would not bring a child into that tenuous situation. With a sigh she tried to set aside her worries.

She turned on her side to run her fingers lightly through his chest hair and stroke him. He was sexy, delightful, exciting—and she was losing him. No matter what she decided to do, she would lose him. If she left for New Mexico, she would lose him now. If she moved in with him, she would lose him later.

What if she moved in with him? She could always move out again if it wasn't working, or they weren't drawing closer. The idea tempted her. Her gaze roamed over him, making her pulse race.

She fell asleep thinking about moving to Dallas and what it would entail. She thought ahead to living there, being with Garrett daily. No one, to her way of thinking, could possibly be as exciting as Garrett was. But then she thought about the years her mother had loved her father, hopelessly. Sophia couldn't move in now with Garrett. She was already doing so many things with him she had said she would never do. Moving in would be the last step, the most disastrous.

It was almost six when she awoke to Garrett showering kisses on her. He soon stepped out of bed and began to gather his clothing. "I have to shower and get back. You have appointments today and so do I."

He left for the shower without asking her to go with him and she felt a separation beginning.

When he was dressed to go, she stood just inside the front door with him while he held her in his arms.

"You've been wonderful all weekend. I think you're going to like knowing the Delaneys. Now you're part of a family."

"It's awesome and mind-boggling. Something I'll have to get accustomed to. I liked all of them. Thank you, Garrett, for getting me to that point."

"You might have gotten there on your own," he said lightly, pulling her closer. "The offer is still open. I want you to move in with me. Don't answer now. Think about it. And I want you to go to Colorado with me next weekend."

She nodded, standing on tiptoe and pulling his head down to kiss him.

Instantly his arms banded her tightly, holding her as close as possible. His kiss ignited passion, branded her as his, became embedded in memory. Shaking, she returned his kiss, trying to convey her feelings in their kisses as much as he had.

"If I had time, we'd be back in bed," he said gruffly. "I'll call you. Go with me next weekend."

"We'll talk," she said solemnly, feeling tears threaten. His gaze searched hers as if he could see her every thought. He turned and left in long, purposeful strides. In seconds he was gone.

"Goodbye, Garrett," she whispered, feeling that she was telling him a final goodbye. In her heart, she felt the budding relationship growing between them was over. Was she ending it? Or would there be this same ending a month or a year from now if she moved in? If that happened, logic indicated a break later, after a long relationship, would be far more devastating than having it happen now. But her heart said a later split with Garrett couldn't cut any deeper than it did now. She wasn't going to move in with him and she needed to make that clear to him.

She closed the door, certain she had ended their relationship. How fragile had it been? How deep did her feelings for him run? Time would tell. It was the first time in her life she had fallen in love. At the moment, she felt like it would be a forever love and that her regret might run incredibly deep.

In a surprising turn of events, she was beginning to have more empathy for her mother, to understand why she had been true to her father all through the years.

As one of his employees approached to park the car, Garrett's cell phone rang. His pulse raced as he answered and hoped it was Sophia with a change of heart.

Garrett tried to hide his disappointment when he heard Edgar's voice.

"Garrett, I haven't talked with Sophia, but I assume all went well in Dallas and her good judgment surfaced?"

"That's right. She's willing to cooperate fully. They all liked each other and got along well."

"She can thank you for getting all this to come about. Thank you for sticking with it when she gave you a difficult time."

"I wanted to for the Delaneys and after I got to know her, for Sophia, as well. She will benefit enormously and now she has a family that really likes her."

"Excellent. I'm glad you're in her life, Garrett. Sophia is a rare gem and deserves someone special. Take care and thanks. I'm greatly relieved."

"Thanks for calling, Edgar," he said.

As he headed for the plane with his thoughts totally on Sophia, he realized he already missed her. He wanted her to live with him. He wanted her where he could be with her daily. How could he entice her to accept his offer?

He flew to Dallas, missing her more with each mile of separation. He had never had a dilemma like this one before. Was he blowing it all out of proportion simply because he wanted her and she had turned him down? It was a first in his life with women.

He entered his Dallas home and for the first time it felt empty. Another first. Sophia had thrown his life into upheaval in too many ways. He swore and called until he found a friend who was free to catch the last half of the Cowboys game.

Twenty minutes into the game from his suite overlooking the field, Garrett realized Sophia had wrapped around his life and he could not shake her out of his thoughts by watching a ball game. He missed her and wanted to be with her. As soon as he got home, he planned to call her.

And say what? What could he say that might change everything for them?

Ten

She was in bed when she heard her cell phone. When she saw Garrett's number, she felt a familiar thrill. "Hi, Garrett," she said, trying to hide her excitement.

"I've been thinking about you constantly since I left you," he said gruffly and her pulse quickened.

"I'm glad you called."

"What have you been doing?"

"Actually, I concluded my appointment about the portrait, and then I haven't done much of anything except get ready for tomorrow." And think about you, she added silently. "What about you?"

"Went to a Cowboys game. They won."

"So you're a Dallas fan?"

"Yes. I barely saw the game. All I could think about was you and wanting to get home where I could call you in private."

Her heart skipped a beat with his answer. "I can't be unhappy with your answer. It's nice to hear your voice."

"This is frustrating. Talking to you causes me to want to be with you more than ever."

"Talking about it makes it even worse."

"I agree. I'll cancel my appointments and fly to Houston early tomorrow if you can cancel your day."

"I can't," she answered regretfully. "I'm leaving for New Mexico."

"Colorado next weekend?" he asked.

She took a deep breath. "Garrett, I'm not going. I'll be in New Mexico for an indefinite time," she said, wondering again if she was making the mistake of her life.

There was silence. "I miss you, Sophia. Really miss you," he repeated in a deeper voice.

"We'll talk when I get back," she said, suspecting that this could be goodbye.

When the call ended, she pulled his picture up on her phone and in minutes was in her studio sketching out a likeness of Garrett.

"I'll have this much of you anyway," she whispered.

She would miss Garrett. The nagging conviction that if she lived with him he might propose disturbed her. Each time she felt that way and succumbed to that belief, she remembered how her mother had felt that way for years, thinking if she did what Argus Delaney wanted, he would marry her. It never happened.

But was Sophia willing to risk losing the only man she had ever loved in order to protect her heart?

Tuesday she flew to New Mexico. She hurt badly over Garrett and missed him more than she had dreamed possible. He hadn't called and she assumed he was breaking things off with her now since she would not live with him.

Wednesday morning she drove to her isolated cabin outside Questa. The caretaker's two dogs came and stayed with her. The afternoons were warm, and the mountain air crisp. She set up her easel to paint outside with the two hounds coming to lie in the sun by her.

She tried to paint, but it was impossible to concentrate. She kept thinking of Garrett, knowing she still could change her mind about moving in with him.

He would soon go to Colorado. She missed him terribly and the nagging knowledge that she could have been with him for another wonderful weekend plagued her. Should she just take chances on life? She could compromise to a degree without moving in, instead of basically cutting him out of her life. Garrett wasn't Argus Delaney or anything like him. She should stop basing her life now on what happened when she was growing up.

She sat in the chair she had placed outside near a tall spruce. She loved Garrett with all her heart, so why not take a chance with him? Life was full of risks—maybe this one was worth taking.

It was worth it. Garrett was worth risking her heart.

Her cabin was out of cell phone range and she usually loved the peace and quiet, but this time, she was restless, steeped in memories of Garrett and missing him every minute until she packed up late Friday and hurried back to Santa Fe, anxious to hear from him.

She discovered she had no messages from him.

Taking off work Garrett flew to Colorado on Wednesday and spent Thursday on the slopes. That night he met friends at a pub, but his heart was not in the evening and he couldn't keep focused on conversations around him. There were women in the group he knew, but he had no interest in even talking to them.

Repeatedly, he reached for his telephone, only to drop it back into his pocket. He missed Sophia far more than he had expected to miss her. What was it about her that made her different from any other woman he had known?

She was beautiful, intelligent, sexy, fun to be with, talented—her own person. Garrett finally said farewell to his friends, grabbed his coat and went back to his place. He built a roaring fire, got a cold beer and sat looking at the flames as he sipped the beer. Was marriage totally out of the question with her?

He had planned to stay single until he was older, putting off a family until later. But why? He was already enormously wealthy as she had pointed out. He loved making furniture. What would happen if he changed his life? He had been a workaholic all his adult life. Will and the Delaneys would manage without him— There were other people capable of doing the job he did.

Sophia had made him look at his life in a different way, to consider the possibilities. The thought of change was exciting, but he could only think about it in terms of her. He wanted her with him if he changed.

Actually, he wanted her with him whatever he did. Marry Sophia whether he stayed at Delaney Enterprises or not. Marry Sophia and have her in his bed every night. Spend his time with her. Was it so impossible? Why not change his timetable? He loved her. He had known he did and tried to ignore how strongly he felt for her. For the first time in his life he was deeply in love.

This week had been pure hell and the thought of her going on her way, finding someone else who would ask her to marry—it was an intolerable notion that made his insides churn.

He grabbed his phone to call her and got nothing. He couldn't leave a message, couldn't even get a ring tone. He tossed his phone across the room and stood up to move closer to the fire while he took a drink of beer. If he had asked her to marry him, she would be with him here now. He drew a deep breath.

He retrieved his phone and called his pilot to see what the weather looked like to fly back to Dallas Friday morning. He couldn't enjoy Colorado and didn't care to stay another night.

After he made arrangements he tried Sophia again and had the same results. He hated being separated from her.

He sat in front of the fire again, thinking about his future and making plans to see her. How long would she be in New Mexico? He had no idea how to find her, but then he realized Edgar might know where the cabin near Questa was located.

Garrett couldn't wait for morning to come. He watched the flames, but saw only images of Sophia, memories spilling through his thoughts of their lovemaking, of being out with her, of dancing with her. He ached to hold her and be with her again and didn't want to spend another weekend like this one.

What was she doing? He couldn't stand to try to guess, hoping she wasn't out with friends the way he had been, meeting guys, seeing some she already knew.

He groaned and tried to think about something else.

He opened his phone and looked at her picture that he loved. That moment had been special, unforgettable. Her hair swirled around her head and she had a huge smile while she looked up with snowflakes on her lashes and cheeks. He wished he had never let her go to New Mexico. How long would she be where he couldn't contact her?

Friday morning he flew back to Dallas, getting in that afternoon. He spent one more night in deep thought about his future. One more night missing Sophia more than ever. During his time away from her, the hurt and loss were growing stronger instead of diminishing.

He had had time for a lot of thought. He wanted Sophia back in his life. Now if he could just convince her and do what he needed to do.

He left his home to drive to downtown Dallas. He had a list of things to do today and one of the first was to call Edgar and find the woman who would be his wife.

Sophia flew home Saturday, arriving in the afternoon. She had had time to think things over away from Garrett. She missed him dreadfully. She showered and changed and then called Garrett on his cell phone.

When he answered, she drew a deep breath. She closed her eyes and thought about him, seeing his gray eyes and locks of brown hair on his forehead.

"Garrett."

"I've tried to call you," he said.

"Sorry, but you can't get through where my cabin is. I'm home now in Houston."

"I'm glad," he said, sounding as if he really meant it.

"I've missed you," she said.

There was a long silence that made her heart lurch and wonder if she had waited too late to call him. "Garrett, I want to talk to you," she said. "And not on the phone. I want to talk in person. What plans do you have?"

"Nothing that can't wait."

"Can we meet somewhere?" she asked. "I can fly to Dallas tonight."

"I think we can find somewhere easier than that."

"I don't mind. I want to talk to you as soon as I can."

"You sound anxious, Sophia," he said.

"I want to see you," she repeated. "Where can we meet?"

"It's not too private, but how about your front door?" he asked, startling her. She leaped up and looked out the front window.

"Garrett!" she cried, dropping the phone and racing downstairs to the front door, throwing it open.

Patiently waiting, looking slightly amused, Garrett lounged against the door frame.

"Garrett," she cried again and grabbed his arm to pull him inside, throwing the door closed as she wrapped her arms around him to kiss him. His leather jacket was cold, but underneath he was warm.

For a fleeting moment he stood still. Frightened that she had waited too late to get back with him, she stilled. Then his arms wrapped tightly around her and he picked her up off her feet.

"Sophia, I've wanted you. I missed you incredibly."

She kissed him, holding him tightly, overjoyed he was in her arms. She leaned away slightly. "Garrett, I was wrong. I should take a chance on us. If you still want me, I'll move in with you and we'll try. I don't want to be alone like I was this week ever again."

"Ahh, Sophia. It's way too late for this moving in business," he said. "I've made my own plans."

"What?" she asked, wondering what he had done during their week apart to make him say such a thing.

Releasing her, he stepped back, reaching into his pocket. Her breath caught. Was he telling her goodbye?

How could he say goodbye and kiss her the way he had? Why was he here if he intended to tell her goodbye?

"Garrett, what—"

He grasped her hand. "Sophia, I love you. Will you marry me?" he asked and held out a dazzling ring.

Eleven

Her heart raced and excitement electrified her. She threw her arms around his neck, hugging him. "Yes, I will. I love you and yes, I will," she said, watching him slip the ring on her finger.

She turned to kiss him and he pulled back slightly. "You're crying."

"Tears of joy," she said, kissing him and ending their talk for a moment.

"Are you home alone?"

"I don't have a staff like you do," she laughed, pulling his head down to continue kissing him. Clothes were tossed aside and in minutes, Garrett picked her up. She locked her long legs around him as she kissed him and they made love passionately.

When she finally stood again, he picked her up and carried her upstairs to her bedroom. As he climbed, she looked at her ring. "I'm impressed with you for carrying me up the stairs. But I'm more impressed with my beautiful, gorgeous, perfect ring. It's wonderful and so are you." She tightened her arms around his neck and smiled at him. "This is paradise. I missed you beyond anything you can imagine."

"I missed you, too," he replied. "I want to marry as soon as possible and then I want to take you on a long honeymoon where I'll have you all to myself. You can't imagine how I missed you, Sophia. I don't want to let you out of my arms."

"Well, you'll have to do that eventually, but hopefully not for too long."

"When would you like to get married?" he asked with a smile.

"Soon. I don't have family to worry about, except the Delaneys, and they won't care what we do."

"They'll help. Let's pick a date. I want to rush this."

"I agree." She looked up at him. "Garrett, how did you know I was home?"

"I was going to fly to New Mexico and go to your cabin to propose. I called Edgar to get directions and he told me you were here."

"I was getting ready to fly to Dallas to see you."

"Then I'm glad we got together before you ended up in Dallas while I was here."

He placed her on her bed and lay beside her, pulling her into his embrace to kiss her again.

Minutes later she slipped off the bed, crossing the room to her closet to get a robe. Finding a calendar, she returned to sit on the bed. He pulled the sheet over his lap and propped himself up beside her.

"Now let's look at dates," she said.

"And then we'll call the Delaneys. I'll ask Will to be my best man."

"I just realized—you don't even know my close friends."

"I look forward to getting to know them. The big question is, how soon can we do this?"

She studied the calendar. "By spending a little more, I imagine I can have a hurry-up wedding. How's two weeks from yesterday? The second of November?"

"I don't want to wait that long, but I will because I want you to have the wedding you want."

"So now I'll live in that castle you call home. I'll need a map."

He laughed. "Tomorrow we can start making plans to build you a studio."

"We'll build me a studio while you think about retiring from Delaney Enterprises and building furniture so we can work at home together."

"We might not get much work done."

"Sure we will. Think about it."

"Actually, I have, a little. I might move it up on my timetable to a few years from now. In the meantime, it's a good hobby."

"If that's what you want. All I want is what makes you happy."

"You make me happy." She looked at him as he talked. His brown hair tumbled in a tangle. He looked fit, strong and handsome. He would soon be her husband—a forever marriage as long as they both would live. Love for him filled her and she placed her hand on his cheek. He stopped talking to focus on her.

"What?"

"I love you, Garrett Cantrell."

"I love you, Mrs. Garrett Cantrell-to-be."

"What happened to your plans to stay single?" she asked, studying him.

He smiled and caressed her cheek. "I met an incredibly beautiful, sexy woman and I had to have her in my life always, so—voilà—marriage."

She laughed and kissed him. When she sat back, she held out her hand to look at her ring, which reflected the light, sparkling brightly. "Garrett, this is the biggest diamond I've ever seen."

"I wanted something to impress you and to please you and to indicate how much you mean to me," he said.

She tossed the calendar on the floor and turned to straddle Garrett as she hugged and kissed him. He playfully shoved her on the bed and rolled over on top of her.

Their wedding plans were temporarily forgotten.

Epilogue

On the second day of November, Sophia stood in the lobby of a huge church filled with guests. The wedding was being held in Dallas since Garrett knew far more people in Dallas than she knew in Houston. The weeks since his proposal had been so busy, she had barely had a moment alone with him. There was a dreamlike quality to the morning. It was strange to think that this was her wedding day.

She carried a bouquet of white orchids and white roses that complemented her plain white satin wedding dress. Edgar had his arm linked with hers and would give the bride away. Before she started down the aisle, he leaned close to speak softly.

"You're ravishing, Sophia, so lovely. I know your mother would be delighted and happy for you."

"Thank you, Edgar," she said, smiling at him.

Trumpets blared and Mendelssohn's "Wedding

March" began. Her gaze went to her tall, handsome husband in his black tux. He took her breath away and she felt as if she were floating down the aisle.

Will was best man while Zach and Ryan, plus two close friends of Garrett's, were groomsmen. Her bridesmaids were all friends, and she had asked Ava to be matron of honor.

The bridesmaids and Ava wore simple pale yellow dresses with spaghetti straps and straight skirts. They carried bouquets of mixed fall flowers.

At the altar, Edgar placed her hand in Garrett's. His warm fingers closed around hers and his gray eyes held love.

They repeated their vows. He kissed her briefly and then they were introduced as man and wife, hurrying back up the aisle together. Her heart pounded with eagerness and joy. She was Garrett's wife, to have and to hold from this day forward. Happiness made her feel radiant.

They patiently posed for pictures and finally left for the country club and the reception. In the limo, Garrett pulled her into his arms to kiss her.

She kissed him, holding him tightly. "I love you, my handsome husband."

"I love you, Sophia. This is wonderful," he said, giving her a squeeze.

They kissed again and then she set about to straightening her dress, despite his best efforts to keep it askew. In minutes they climbed out and joined the reception.

Garrett had the first dance with Sophia. She still felt as if she were floating on air. "I can't stop smiling, Garrett. This is the happiest day of my life." He held her lightly, and she longed to touch his hair, brush it back in place, but she kept her hands to herself.

"I'm glad. I can say the same. You're stunning, Sophia. I have the most beautiful bride ever."

She laughed. "I know you're biased or blind, but I'm glad you feel that way."

"I wish my parents had known you, and known about our marriage. That would have pleased both of them. Dad would have been impressed by your business sense. Mom would have loved you."

"I'm sorry I didn't know them, too. And my mother would have been so happy because I'm happy."

"And very married. No danger of you being treated the way Argus treated her."

She smiled at her handsome husband and thought how wonderful to be married to the man she loved.

The music ended and she danced the next dance with Edgar.

"I'm happy for you, Sophia. This is truly wonderful and I like Garrett. I heartily approve."

"I'm glad, Edgar. I love him very much. How do you like my new family?"

"They're nice men and I think they are delighted to find you and have you marry their friend."

"I hope so."

She glanced across the room to see Garrett talking to the Delaneys. They were all handsome men. Zach had rugged looks, but his riveting blue eyes were as distinctive as Garrett's gray ones. Ryan was laughing at something one of them said. She was thankful that she had changed her mind— She had some wonderful half brothers now. The more she got to know them, the more she liked them, and Ava was quickly becoming a good friend.

Later, Will asked her to dance. As they began to move across the floor, he smiled at her. "We are all happy for you and for Garrett. We had to push and argue to get him to meet you for us, so this justifies our actions."

Smiling, she knew Will was teasing. "Now I'm glad you did. It's been wonderful to get to know all of you."

"Good. You're getting a great guy for a husband."

She glanced across the dance floor to see Garrett talking to Ava. "I know I am. I love him more than I thought possible."

"I wish you all the happiness in the world," Will said.

"Thank you," she replied, smiling at him.

"I see your new husband headed this way."

She danced with Garrett and then Ryan appeared at her elbow to ask her to dance. Unable to dance because of injuring his foot, Zach had given her a toast earlier. Now he sat on the sidelines while he talked to friends.

It was late in the afternoon when Garrett finally took her arm. "I've told the guys goodbye. If you're okay with Edgar, I'd say let's go."

"That's what I've been waiting to hear," she said, smiling at him, her heart racing at the thought of being alone with him.

"Come with me. I know the best escape route and we have a limo waiting." He took her arm and they left through the kitchen. Garrett spoke to each person they passed in the kitchen, calling them by name.

They rushed to the limo and soon were on their way to the airport. They flew in Garrett's private jet to New York City to spend the night. On board she changed to a tan suit and matching pumps. As soon as they were in their suite in New York, Garrett turned to take her into his arms.

"I love you, Mrs. Cantrell."

"I love you beyond measure, Garrett."

He nuzzled her neck. He raised his head to look at her, smiling with love filling his expression. She wrapped her arms around his neck and held him tightly while her joy was overwhelming. She loved her handsome husband with all her being and was ready to begin a life with Garrett that she expected to be filled with happiness.

* * * * *

COMING NEXT MONTH from Harlequin Desire®
AVAILABLE SEPTEMBER 4, 2012

#2179 UP CLOSE AND PERSONAL
Maureen Child

He's danger. She's home and hearth. So the red-hot affair between a California beauty and an Irish rogue ends too soon. But then he returns, wanting to know what she's been hiding....

#2180 A SILKEN SEDUCTION
The Highest Bidder
Yvonne Lindsay

A hotshot art expert seduces an important collection out of a lonely heiress, but their night of passion quickly leads to pregnancy and a marriage of convenience.

#2181 WHATEVER THE PRICE
Billionaires and Babies
Jules Bennett

A Hollywood director's marriage is on the rocks when he gains custody of his orphaned niece. Now he'll do anything to keep his wife...and the baby she's carrying!

#2182 THE MAID'S DAUGHTER
The Men of Wolff Mountain
Janice Maynard

When this billionaire offers the maid's daughter a job, it leads to an affair that reveals the secrets of his traumatic past.

#2183 THE SHEIKH'S CLAIM
Desert Knights
Olivia Gates

When the woman who ignites his senses becomes the mother of his child, nothing can stop him from laying claim to his heir—and her heart.

#2184 A MAN OF DISTINCTION
Sarah M. Anderson

Returning home for the case of his career, a wealthy Native American lawyer must choose between winning in court and reuniting with the love he left behind—and the child she kept a secret.

You can find more information on upcoming Harlequin® titles, free excerpts and more at www.Harlequin.com.

HDCNM0812

REQUEST YOUR FREE BOOKS!
2 FREE NOVELS PLUS 2 FREE GIFTS!

Harlequin®

Desire

ALWAYS POWERFUL, PASSIONATE AND PROVOCATIVE

YES! Please send me 2 FREE Harlequin Desire® novels and my 2 FREE gifts (gifts are worth about $10). After receiving them, if I don't wish to receive any more books, I can return the shipping statement marked "cancel." If I don't cancel, I will receive 6 brand-new novels every month and be billed just $4.30 per book in the U.S. or $4.99 per book in Canada. That's a saving of at least 14% off the cover price! It's quite a bargain! Shipping and handling is just 50¢ per book in the U.S. and 75¢ per book in Canada.* I understand that accepting the 2 free books and gifts places me under no obligation to buy anything. I can always return a shipment and cancel at any time. Even if I never buy another book, the two free books and gifts are mine to keep forever.

225/326 HDN FEF3

Name	(PLEASE PRINT)

Address	Apt. #

City	State/Prov.	Zip/Postal Code

Signature (if under 18, a parent or guardian must sign)

Mail to the **Reader Service:**
IN U.S.A.: P.O. Box 1867, Buffalo, NY 14240-1867
IN CANADA: P.O. Box 609, Fort Erie, Ontario L2A 5X3

Not valid for current subscribers to Harlequin Desire books.

Want to try two free books from another line?
Call 1-800-873-8635 or visit www.ReaderService.com.

* Terms and prices subject to change without notice. Prices do not include applicable taxes. Sales tax applicable in N.Y. Canadian residents will be charged applicable taxes. Offer not valid in Quebec. This offer is limited to one order per household. All orders subject to credit approval. Credit or debit balances in a customer's account(s) may be offset by any other outstanding balance owed by or to the customer. Please allow 4 to 6 weeks for delivery. Offer available while quantities last.

Your Privacy—The Reader Service is committed to protecting your privacy. Our Privacy Policy is available online at www.ReaderService.com or upon request from the Reader Service.

We make a portion of our mailing list available to reputable third parties that offer products we believe may interest you. If you prefer that we not exchange your name with third parties, or if you wish to clarify or modify your communication preferences, please visit us at www.ReaderService.com/consumerchoice or write to us at Reader Service Preference Service, P.O. Box 9062, Buffalo, NY 14269. Include your complete name and address.

HDES11B

Enjoy this sneak peek of USA TODAY *bestselling author*
Maureen Child's newest title
UP CLOSE AND PERSONAL

Available September 2012 from Harlequin® Desire!

"Laura, I know you're in there!"

Ronan Connolly pounded on the bright blue front door,
then paused to listen. Not a sound from inside the house,
though he knew too well that Laura was in there. Hell, he
could practically *feel* her standing just on the other side of
the damned door.

He glanced at her car parked alongside the house, then
glared again at the still-closed front door.

"You won't convince me you're not at home. Your car is
parked in the street, Laura."

Her voice came then, muffled but clear. "It's a driveway
in America, Ronan. You're not in Ireland, remember?"

"More's the pity." He scrubbed one hand across his face
and rolled his eyes in frustration. If they were in Ireland
right now, he'd have half the village of Dunley on his side
and he'd bloody well get her to open the door.

"I heard that," she said.

Grinding his teeth together, he counted to ten. Then did
it a second time. "Whatever the hell you want to call it,
Laura, your car is *here* and so are you. Why not open the
door and we can talk this out. Together. In private."

"I've got nothing to say to you."

He laughed shortly. That would be a first indeed, he told
himself. A more opinionated woman he had never met. He
had to admit, he had enjoyed verbally sparring with her. He
admired a quick mind and a sharp tongue. He'd admired her
even more once he'd gotten her into his bed.

HDEXP0912

He glanced down at the dozen red roses he held clutched in his right hand and called himself a damned fool for thinking this woman would be swayed by pretty flowers and a smooth speech. Hell, she hadn't even *seen* the flowers yet. At this rate, she never would.

Huffing out an impatient breath, he lowered his voice. "You know why I'm here. Let's get it done and have it over then."

There was a moment's pause, as if she were thinking about what he'd said. Then she spoke up again. "You can't have him."

"What?"

"You heard me."

Ronan narrowed his gaze fiercely on the door as if he could see through the panel to the woman beyond. "Aye, I heard you. Though, I don't believe it. I've come for what's mine, Laura, and I'm not leaving until I have it."

Will Ronan get what he's come for?

Find out in Maureen Child's new title
UP CLOSE AND PERSONAL

Available September 2012 from Harlequin® Desire!

HARLEQUIN®

SYtyCW
SO YOU THINK YOU CAN WRITE

Harlequin and Mills & Boon are joining
forces in a global search for new authors.

In September 2012 we're launching our
biggest contest yet—with the prize of
being published by the world's leader
in romance fiction!

Look for more information on our website,
www.soyouthinkyoucanwrite.com

So you think you can write? Show us!